# Sanitarium Magazine
# Issue no. 11

First Published 2013 by Sanitarium Press

This edition published 2020 by Sanitarium Publishing


ISBN: 9798693612167




Facebook: https://www.facebook.com/SanitariumPublishing


2013 Edition edited by Barry Skelhorn

2020 Edition by Ian Sputnik

*Thank you to all of our contributors, we couldn't have done it without you.*

# Contents

ISSUE ELEVEN

As I write this introduction, from my window I can see a strange fiery ball in the sky. For us in Blighty this is a rare and wonderful thing - summer is here at last. No Pagan rituals were needed, only a little patience. BBQs up and down the land are being dusted off, scrubbed down and painstakingly lit.

With all of this time in the sun surely people's reading tastes would change? Gone is the blood lust and gore craving, only to be replaced with trashy holiday reading by the pool or on the beach....
Oh no, not you lot!

I had the chance to sit down and speak with a few writers and fans of horror literature and movies. The talk over the BBQ moved quickly onto what's going to be the next big thing? Who's reading what and what would they recommend for the next read?

Summer may only be for a few weeks of the year (again this is British weather I'm talking about) but as a good friend said.... Horror is for life! Until next issue.

Welcome to the Sanitarium.

Barry Skelhorn

# On the Farm

## Joshua D. Thomas

Physician: Dr. Roundtree
8245-AVD12

id ca
etails
that w
her fla
was a y
was that
never

It had rained steadily since dawn, cold February rain. When the rain stopped, just after dark, it was as sudden as if someone had turned a faucet off. Steve walked onto his porch, a cigarette dangling from one corner of his mouth, just in time to watch the fog roll in. It came like something alive, so thick that the streetlight above his driveway was just a faint ember in the gloom.

Steve sat down in his grandfather's rocking chair, hand built from oak in the '50's. Frankie, his redbone hound, came trotting onto the porch and looked up at him with pleading eyes. Sighing, Steve tipped his bottle of beer and poured a little out onto the porch. Frankie lapped up the beer and then lay down at Steve's feet, content with his nightcap.

Steve sat in the rocking chair, moisture from the fog soaking his face, until the howls split the night. The howls came almost every night, but in rainy weather, it seemed that whatever gave voice to the eerie cries was more active. Frankie raised his head off the porch and looked at Steve.

"Let's go in the house boy." Steve told the dog.

As if he understood, Frankie jumped up and went to the door, looking back impatiently at Steve until he opened it. The dog ran in ahead and lay down by the stove, warming himself by its heat. Steve bolted the door behind him and put another good-sized log into the stove. After getting another beer from the fridge, he sat down in his arm chair and picked up the pistol laying on the table beside him. He opened the cylinder on the big .44 magnum, reassuring himself that it was fully loaded with hollow points. Laying the pistol down on his lap, he settled back into his chair to wait out another long night.

The howls split the night again, closer this time, and chills ran up and down Steve's spine. For nearly three months, almost nightly, he'd sat here in this chair, pistol in his lap and his father's .300 Weatherby Magnum leaning within arms-reach in the corner. Whatever was out there would come onto his property and take what it pleased. Sometimes he'd go out in the morning and one of his goats would be gone, but usually it was a hog. So far, it hadn't gotten one of his horses, but Steve didn't know whether that was because it had no taste for horseflesh or because he always shut them up in the barn at night. Either way, the hogs were nearly gone, and the number of his goats had been cut in half. Soon, he feared, he'd know the answer to that particular question.

He felt like a coward, hiding inside his house while the thing ravaged the land that three generations of his family had worked. On the first night, when he heard the pigs squealing, he'd gone out with his .12-gauge pump, expecting to find a coyote in the pig pen. He'd seen something, a confusing mass of dark fur revealed in his flashlight beam, and fired at it. The shotgun had been loaded with double-ought buckshot; a load that should make even a bear reconsider its actions. Steve heard the heavy *thump* of the pellets hitting home, and the creature whirled on him. He couldn't make out what the thing looked like, he saw only a blur of teeth and claws and cold blue eyes that seemed to burn with their own light.

Steve chambered another round and fired again. The animal fell to the ground, but immediately leaped back to its feet. Firing once more, Steve turned and ran back to the house, sweeping the heavy wooden door closed behind him just before something slammed into it. He grabbed the .300 Weatherby mag. from the gun rack. The rifle was always loaded, and Steve turned back toward the door, working the bolt. For several long moments, he heard only silence form the porch, and when he looked out the window, found it empty. That's when, from what sounded like a long distance, the creature cut loose with the first of those terrifying howls.

After that night, Steve had been unable to work up the courage to confront the creature again. This night, like so many others, he sat in his chair and listened, finally dozing off a couple of hours before dawn. When he woke, bright sunlight was visible around the edges of the window curtains. He went to the bathroom to empty his bladder, and then strapped his gun belt on and slid the big Ruger Redhawk into its holster. Calling for Frankie he went out the front door to survey the damage to his dwindling livestock, the dog following at his heels.

It had gone for the goats this time, pieces of his black billy were strewn about the pen, and all three of the month-old kids were gone. The five-foot high fence was perfectly intact, as it always was after an attack. Whatever it was, it always jumped the fence in and out, sometimes carrying a couple of full-grown goats with it. Steve fed the goats and calmed them the best he could, then did the rest of his round. None of the pigs had been touched, and the horses were still secure in their stalls.

After letting the horses out to graze, Steve went inside. He ate a light breakfast of eggs and toast, showered and dressed. With Frankie following along, he got into his International Harvester pickup and headed for town. Town was Harper Springs, 20 miles away. Steve lived down a deserted stretch of dirt road called Whiskey Hollow Road, his closest neighbor was almost ten miles away, at the very head of the road. He only went into town about once a month to stock up on supplies. Even before these latest troubles, Steve had liked to keep to himself.

A couple miles from the farm, Steve brought the truck to a stop. Several thick trees had fallen across the road, completely blocking it off. With a big drop-off on one side and a steep hill on the other, there was no hope of going around. Steve looked over at Frankie, who looked back at him intently.

"Ok," he said. "We'll go back and get the chainsaw, cut this shit up and get it out of the way."

He went home and fetched his Stihl saw, came back to the trees and went to work. It took better than two hours for him to realize that it was useless. The trees were piled up over his head in some places, and every time he started to make headway with one of them, the pile collapsed and filled the hole. It would take the work of several days to clear this mess by himself. Steve gave up and headed back to the house.

He sat on the porch, but the temperature was dropping steadily, and just before full dark it began to snow. Inside, he stoked the fire and sat down to clean his guns. As he oiled the .300, he thought back to the many hunting trips he and his father had gone on. In those days, there had been more money, and the two men had hunted most of the country, the highlight of which were two trips to Alaska. On the first trip, Steve had taken a caribou with this very rifle. The second trip had been in the springtime, and his father had killed a huge brown bear with the big .416 Remington that hung on the rack above Steve's head. That was all before his father's bout with cancer four years earlier.

His thoughts were interrupted by a loud, splintering crash from outside. Steve jumped to his feet, clutching the freshly reloaded rifle. Outside, the horses were whinnying in terror and a long, loud howl split the night. Close, it was very close.

"Not the horses," Steve cried, flipping on the outside light and rushing outside, heedless of his fear.

About two inches of snow had accumulated and it was still pouring down, driven by hard winds. He ran around the side of the house, and stopped short 15 feet from the barn. The floodlight attached to the side of the house lit everything in perfect detail. There was the creature, crouched on top of one of the horses, snarling and tearing at it. Finally seeing it, he was first struck by just how big the thing was. It was a massive wall of black fur, with a long bushy tail waving back and forth behind it.

He shouldered the rifle and fired. The thing let out a high-pitched scream and tumbled to the ground. It rolled on the ground for a moment and then rose to its feet, and Steve stopped in the middle of working the rifle bolt. The thing stood on two thick legs, towering over Steve, who was six feet three inches tall. Dumbstruck, he thought it must be over eight feet tall. It had the bulk of a Kodiak bear but the frame of a man, with thinner hair around it's muscular chest and stomach. The head sitting on those massive shoulders was like a nightmare. Wolf was the first thing that popped into Steve's mind, with its long, toothy snout and canine ears. But it bore only the vaguest structural resemblance to a wolf, like a prehistoric ancestor to modern canines, primal and untamed.

Its cold blue eyes bored into his own, and Steve slammed the bolt home. He sighted on the beast's chest and fired. It stumbled backward, screaming, and he shot it again in the abdomen. Chambering another round, Steve stepped forward, intent on finishing it, when one of the horses ran between him and the creature. The mare only blocked his view for a split second, but when she was past, the creature was gone. Trying to look in every direction at once, Steve backed toward the house, only one cartridge left in the rifle. He put his back against the side of the house and slid along the wall until he reached the porch, then he ran into the house and slammed the door behind him.

Frankie was just inside the door, barking, clearly agitated. Steve crouched down and petted the dog, who licked his face and growled reproachfully, as if resentful of being left out of the action. Steve walked over and took his father's .416 down from the gun rack, got a box of ammunition from the desk in the corner, and loaded the big rifle. He sat down in his chair, smoking a cigarette and staring at the door, expecting the beast to come crashing through it at any moment.

It never happened though, and he passed the night staring at the door and smoking cigarettes until his throat was dry and raw. Just before dawn, a single long howl split the silence, but nothing followed. When Steve thought it was bright enough outside, he left his post and began preparing for the night to come.

The snow continued until around noon, the clouds parted shortly after and the sun came out. The temperature didn't rise enough to melt much of the snow, which was nearly six inches deep. Steve gathered up the horses and put them back into their pens inside the barn. After feeding the other animals, he went inside and went to sleep on his bed.

His alarm clock went off at 4:30 p.m., and he went into the kitchen. He cooked some hamburgers for himself and Frankie, both of them ate ravenously. After eating, Steve dressed in insulated Carhartt bibs with a thick long-sleeved shirt and his heavy boots. The bibs would allow his upper body a better range of movement than his usual heavy coveralls. He put on his gun belt, the big .44 a reassuring weight on his hip, and picked up his father's .416. The rifle only held three rounds, but the caliber was widely used for dangerous game in Africa. Steve was confident that, if anything could kill the beast, this rifle would do the trick.

With night closing fast, he walked out into the yard, with Frankie following close behind. On the side of the house, where last night's encounter had taken place, Steve had piled up a large stack of firewood earlier in the day. He doused the stack with some kerosene and lit it. By the time darkness had fallen, a sizable bonfire was burning. A single howl split the night, and in it, he heard an edge that hadn't been there before. It sounded like rage.

Steve kept his back to the fire, as close as he could stand, so there would be no chance of the thing sneaking up behind him. He waited, smoking cigarettes and wanting a beer. That was a luxury he would not allow himself, because he knew full well one would quickly turn into six. He needed to be as sharp as possible, couldn't afford to lose a fraction of his reaction time. As he waited, his fear began to build. He had to admit that he was terrified. But he felt no shame because of this. Any man with even a hint of intelligence would be afraid. He was no story book hero; he was just a farmer who drank too much and smoked too many cigarettes. Nonetheless, he would not give in to that fear. He would make his stand, and try to stay alive to see the sunrise.

No more howls came, and Steve was beginning to wonder if it was going to come at all when the horses started whinnying in their stalls. Frankie jumped to his feet, growling and staring off into the darkness, lips pulled back from his teeth. Steve saw the flash of cold blue eyes a moment before the beast stepped within reach of the firelight. It came slowly, on all fours, sniffing the air. It seemed hesitant, possibly frightened by the fire.

Steve raised the rifle to his shoulder, and the creature tensed, baring its massive teeth and growling. He pulled the trigger an instant before the wolf-thing charged. The recoil was brutal, but the slug, which was adequate to put down an elephant, was definitely effective. Steve had missed its head, but the creature's left shoulder exploded in a mess of bone and blood and fur. The beast fell to the ground, then jumped up and came on, impossibly fast, the left arm held tight against its chest. Steve, desperately trying to chamber another round, snapped the bolt closed an instant before the beast slammed into him.

The impact knocked him sprawling, the breath jarred from his body. Pain flared in his left arm as it struck one of the burning logs behind him. The beast continued over top of him and, a split second after Steve hit the ground, slammed headlong into the bonfire. Flaming logs scattered everywhere and the smell of burning hair filled the night. Scrabbling backward, away from the deadly rain, Steve reached for the .44. Before he could pull it, the beast was on top of him again, parts of its fur still flaming.

In desperation, Steve threw his burned left arm up as the dripping jaws descended. He caught a handful of fur and held on, screaming in pain as the jaws savaged his forearm. Pinned under the immense weight, he was unable to pull the pistol. Gripped with panic, he stared up into those cold blue eyes. He gagged on its hot, stinking breath, and knew he was about to die. He felt heat in his crotch and knew that his bladder had let go. The jaws yawned, wide enough to engulf his entire head. But they never closed.

The wolf-thing shrieked and Steve felt some of the weight raise off him. Frankie had his jaws locked on a dangling piece of meat on the thing's wounded shoulder and was tearing at it viciously.

The beast lashed out with its jaws, and Frankie went rolling away, squealing in pain. With the bulk temporarily off his chest, Steve pulled the .44 from its holster and shoved the barrel against the thing's thick neck. He fired all six of the hollow point rounds into it and the beast rolled off of him.

He saw the rifle to his left and lunged for it, screaming as hot lines of agony tore across his right thigh and buttock. Steve turned onto his back and saw the thing coming again, slowly, its chest covered with blood. He jammed the rifle barrel into those dripping, tooth filled jaws and pulled the trigger. A shower of hot blood, bits of stinging bone and thicker stuff splashed across his face. The wolf-thing fell and was finally still. Steve poked it with the rifle, got no response, and promptly passed out.

When he came to, it was still dark, and he was stiff with cold. Logs still burned here and there across the yard, but by some miracle, none of them had caught the house up. Frankie was lying beside him, covered in blood but breathing. Suddenly, it came back to him, and he scrambled to his feet, heedless of the agony in his arm and leg. When his eyes fell on the dead beast laying at his feet, his mouth dropped open in shock.

A man lay before him, thin and completely naked. He didn't recognize the man, but since there was no head to speak of, that wasn't surprising. Frankie had gotten to his feet and gave the body a quick sniff, then turned and walked slowly toward the porch.

Steve grabbed the body by the right arm, the left one was attached only by a thin string of skin. He dragged the body over to the bonfire, where a sizable stack of logs still burned. With some effort, he laid the body on top and then doused it with the remainder

of the kerosene. Having no interest in watching the man burn, he walked into the house to tend to his wounds.

His left arm was torn down to the bone in places, but the bleeding had mostly stopped, so he didn't think it was life threatening. Wincing in pain, he doused the arm in peroxide and then wrapped it in a bandage. There were nasty tears across the back of his right thigh and buttock, but he couldn't reach them to properly bandage them. So, he cleaned them up the best he could and put on some loose jogging pants. There was a half full bottle of Vicodin in his medicine cabinet, left over from a broken arm a couple years before. He washed four of them down with a beer from the refrigerator and checked on Frankie.

The dog had lost his left eye and most of the ear on that side. Steve cleaned the ear up and wrapped a bandage around Frankie's head to cover the eye. He'd have to get the dog to the vet, but he didn't have the strength to clean up the mess on the road yet. After some sleep, Steve decided, he'd do what he had to do. Frankie was not going to lay up here and die of an infection in his eye.

Steve went into his bedroom, loading the Ruger and taking it with him, although he didn't think the wolf-thing would be coming back. Sleeping with a pistol on the table beside him had always been a habit. He slept all that day, waking that night with a raging fever. A thermometer wasn't necessary; Steve knew what a fever felt like. He needed to use the bathroom, but was too dizzy to get out of bed, so he simply fell back asleep.

Sometime later, he was startled awake by a loud crash. He sat up in bed and turned on the lamp. Standing in his doorway was a wolf, rusty red in color and the size of a pony. Steve grabbed the pistol from the table and took aim. One burning blue eye stared at him coldly as the wolf crouched, growling low in its throat.

The wolf leaped, and the revolver bucked in Steve's hand. Minutes later, Steve sat looking at Frankie lying dead on the floor.

The fever raged through him, and he cried out in pain as he felt his body swelling outward. The cracking sounds were deafening as his bones re-knit themselves into strange, new shapes. His screams of agony rose in volume, ending in a long, loud howl that split the night.


The End.

# The Guest

## Nathaniel Brehmer

Physician: Dr. Peterson
8268-WCT29

In life, everything comes down to the choices we make.

Choices are what define us. They are what allow us to change. Sometimes for the better, sometimes for the worse. It was the last summer before college. We had already started drifting apart but were still at the stage where no one wanted to admit it. Why would we? We knew we weren't having the time of our lives, but we felt this was as close as we would ever get. Who knew what college would bring? All we knew was that we would be away from each other, and for most of us, that was enough.

I was driving the car. My name is Alex. Alongside me were the three people I could most comfortably call friends. Paul was my best friend since Elementary school, and we were almost surprised that we stuck so close together through high school. Simple reasoning, really, he got popular and I didn't. But our bond was close, and even at his most infuriating, the guy is like a brother to me. Our other closest friend, and the guy who will be Paul's roommate when they go off to college, was Stevie Holster. He was sort of a weird kid, but funny and nice, and we liked him. Maybe we were just more tolerant than other kids, because they only seemed to want Stevie around in fairly small doses.

Then, finally, her hair shimmering in the sunlight in my rear-view mirror... there was Sophie. I had been in love with her since freshman year; somehow it felt even longer than that. Ageless, almost. Over time, we became pretty close friends, but even then... even when we were about to graduate, I had never mustered up the balls to actually ask her out. Explain to her how I really felt. Paul and Stevie both knew and tried to help me as much as they could. They were my best friends. What else could they do? I appreciated their help, I really did. But no matter what they said, I still had never been able to do it. I had never been able to say a damn thing to her. Worse even, because all I wanted to do was tell her I loved her, it made me unable to speak to her at all sometimes, and we were starting to drift as friends.

Before we went on that drive, decided to have one last weekend at my parents' cabin before we all left, Paul had come up to me and reminded me that if I really cared about Sophie, this was my final chance to tell her. After this… who knew what could happen? All that was certain was the fact that I had to act and do something, anything, before I ended up spending my entire life wondering about what could have been.

I hadn't driven to the cabin on my own ever. I had only ever gone with my parents, and for most of that time I was usually passed out in the back. I tend to do that, sleep in the car. It's not like they usually had much of anything interesting to say as it was. Stevie, somehow, could sense that I was struggling with the directions in my head, and leaned forward to tap me on the shoulder.

"Do you even know where we're going?" he asked.

"It's my parent's cabin," I said, sort of replying without actually replying.

"So, you have no clue, then."

Steering with one hand, I raised my other in protest. "No. I do have an idea. It's just sort of a vague idea. Normally, my parents drive and I sleep on these adventures. I'm going from memory, and memory's pretty shaky."

"Why didn't you just ask them to borrow the GPS?" Paul asked. I sighed. "Because they love that thing more than any of their children," I said, then added, "and I'm not really sure how to program it."

"So, we're lost?" Sophie asked.

"No, we're not lost," I assured her. "We stay on the main road for most of the way. There are only a few turns when we get to the nearest town. It's really not that hard to navigate. Even an idiot like me could do it."

"Well," she said. "That is a comfort."

Ouch. I don't know why, because friends tease each other all the time, but it hurt when it came from her. Maybe that was something inside me waking up and trying to tell me that I didn't have a chance in hell.

Maybe.

We talked a little and drove in silence for even longer. I recognized when we were getting close by the cemetery. For whatever reason, when I came up here with my parents, I would always wake up just outside that cemetery. It was not what one would expect from a cemetery in central Maine, especially not in a town this small. For one, the thing was huge. It was the size of a great field; only instead of cows there were corpses, buried down under the frozen earth. Even in the heat of summer, the ground seemed stagnant and frozen in there. That was another weird thing.

But the weirdest thing, easily, was the state of it. The fence had rotted away. The gravestones were decaying, covered in moss, and the tool shed had collapsed in on itself—looked like it had caved in a while ago. Everywhere I looked, every time I drove by there, it all suggested the same thing to me: this cemetery looked like it hadn't been touched in years. Not by anyone. Even all the flowers had decayed and rotted away, only stems remained, if even that.

"Isn't that weird?" I suggested to Paul, but he shrugged. "How is it weird?"

"Well," I said, "I mean it doesn't look like the place has been touched by anyone in years, even visited. People still have relatives, right? And people still have to die, I know that. People still live in this town. But it doesn't look like anyone gets buried anymore, or like anyone even works here. How is that possible? Why would they let a whole cemetery just sit and rot like this?"

"I don't know," he said, turning over to look out the opposite window. "Keep your eyes on the road."

I did. I didn't bring up the cemetery again, but it didn't leave my mind.

Sophie didn't say anything, but I could tell as she looked out at it that she was wondering the same thing.

After a few minutes, we came to the fork in the road—the one that I had been secretly dreading for miles. I had never remembered this part of the drive, and my dad didn't give me anything to go on when I asked to be reminded of the directions. There was Warwick Drive and Rosemary Way, and I could never remember which direction was the right one. It's funny how the biggest choices we make in life can, at the time, appear so small.

We never plan things, not really. We pretend that we are in control of our lives, but we never are.

The point is, when I came to that fork in the road and I was presented with that choice, I chose Rosemary Way.

It was the wrong choice.

When we drove down it, almost the second we turned down that road, it started getting dark. The lake (Bell Lake, where my cabin sat waiting) stretched around both roads. One road went along one side, the other road on the other side. It was a very big lake. I didn't think much of it at the time, but in the early evening, a mist started to rise off the water. The further we drove, the more trees stood between the lake and us, until eventually we just couldn't see it anymore.

Now, I know everything that happened that night was my fault. There's no way I would try to deny that now, even if no one believes it happened at all. I am going to deal with the memory for the rest of my life, and carry the burden that I am responsible. Having said that, we were on that road—clearly the wrong road—for a half hour before any of them said anything to me. You would think that one of them would bring it up, before it got too late. Too dark.

Instead, Stevie just tapped my shoulder again and said. "You know we're lost, right?" in that annoying, thinks-he's-helpful tone.

"Yeah. I've figured that out."

"Well, what are we going to do?" Sophie asked. "It's a half hour back to the other road. You really should have planned this out better."

Again, ouch.

"I know," I said. All I could say, really. I turned back to give something more than an apology, but instead I just saw three sets of widening eyes, all of them turning to me and screaming in unison:

"Look out!"

I looked ahead. Illuminated in the headlights was a dark shape. That was interesting, in retrospect. The thing stood in the headlights, and yet it was not lit up. It didn't get any shine from the lights at all, the dark shape was still a dark shape, until we slammed into it and sent it into the woods on the side of the road. Two people screaming behind me, and I brought the car to a stop.

We all got out. There was a dent in my car. No blood on it, and I took that as a good sign.

"What did we hit?" Sophie asked, stepping out. "Did we hit a person?"

"I don't know," I said, looking around. "They fell off the hood, couldn't have gotten far." But as I said that, I didn't see any sign of whoever—or whatever—it was that we had smashed into. We? No, once again, this was my fault.

"What are we going to do?" Stevie asked.

"Call the police," Paul said, matter-of-factly. I always admired how he kept his mind straight, even when things got rough. Hell, even when he was high. He always knew the right thing to do. "We'll call the police and tell them what happened, tell them we hit something, don't know what it was, don't know if it was a person and we can't find them either way. Nothing to freak out about. They probably get calls like this all the time. It could have just been a deer, anyway. Better safe than sorry."

"He's right," I said.

"There's only one problem," Sophie said flatly. "My phone doesn't work, how about you guys?"

I hadn't even stopped to think about that, but she had a point. "This whole area is cut off by the mountains, the whole town at least. There's no cell service for miles."

"Great," Stevie said. "Now what?"

I looked at Paul for the answer, but he was looking right back at me. "Alright," I said, trying to think of something. "There has to be a house around here. We'll just drive until we find a house, then ask to use their phone."

Paul nodded. "It's a plan."

I didn't know then how much I would grow to hate that word, so we all got back in the car and started to drive. Ten minutes of nothing but building anxiety and silent tension before we saw a house. It was small, two story yellow house, looked like it could have belonged to any grandmother in rural Maine. The place looked, in a word, innocent. So, we parked on the other side of the road and got out.

I went up there first. It was, after all, my fault, so it was only fair. The others followed behind me. I knocked on the door. At first there was nothing, no answer, so I knocked again. Then, I heard a sweet voice from the other side say, "hold your horses, dears, I'm coming."

The door opened and a small, withered old woman answered. She smiled at me, then at the others. "Oh, no, look at you poor distressed kids. What seems to be the trouble?"

"It's our car… we think we hit something, but we're not sure. Could we use your phone to call the police?"

"Oh, you poor things *must* be stressed. Now, please, come in. My husband and my granddaughter are here, lonely old souls like me; they'd love the company. You just all come on in and sit down. I'll put some tea on."

She moved inside, expecting us to do the same, so we did. After we were all in, I asked, "So, you will let us use your phone, then?" She turned. "Oh, no, no, dears me. Our phone broke a long time ago, and we always meant to get another one, but we just never did. So we can't help you with that, but please do sit down. I'll put the tea on and go and get my husband. You kids rest here, you must have had a rough trip. There's more than plenty of room, you know. You could stay here tonight and figure this mess out in the morning."

"Please," I said, "that's very sweet of you, but we really should get this figured out. If you could at least tell us how to get to the police station so that we could report this ourselves, we'd really appreciate that."

"Oh, nonsense. You kids worry too much. God, you'll be all wrinkled like me just from the stress if you keep this up."

Just like that, she disappeared into the kitchen and we stood there, dazed, before we heard someone coming down the stairs. Even though I was in love with the girl breathing against my back, the girl that came down over those stairs was the most beautiful thing I had ever seen. Stevie saw it more clearly than any of us. His mouth was hanging open, drooling, like a big dumb dog. The girl smiled sweetly.

"I didn't realize we had company," she said. "My name's Charlotte."

"This is Stevie," Stevie said. "I mean… I am Stevie. That's me."

"Paul," Paul said, extending his hand, slightly more charming.

But Charlotte seemed somehow more intrigued by Stevie's bumbling.

"Nice to meet you all," she said. "Please sit down."

She did, and we did. Eventually, the old woman returned with her husband. "Oh, my, I didn't make proper introductions," she said. "I'm Edna Mae. This is my husband, Rick. And you've already met Charlotte, I presume."

"How do you do?" Rick asked, scarily polite.

"We're fine. We're all fine, thank you. Do you know, sir, where the police station is? We really should get down there."

"You kids shouldn't be going anywhere, not at this hour. I'm sure my wife has already told you that. I could see from the window that you got a nasty dent on your hood. That, well, that I might actually be able to help with."

"You know," Edna Mae said, "with all of this, I forgot to check on the tea." She turned to Sophie and Charlotte. "Would you girls mind giving me a hand in the kitchen?" she asked, smiling.

"Certainly not," Sophie said politely. I was always amazed by how sweet she could be in any given situation.

Rick turned to Stevie, Paul and me. "And you boys," he said, "can give me a hand down in the cellar. We could get a few things sorted out for your car, teach you kids a valuable lesson or two."

"Sure," I said. "That would be great."

We followed him to the basement door. He opened it up, there was an old wooden staircase, hand-made, but we couldn't see very far past that. There was nothing down there that I could see, but I could *smell* something very clearly. Whatever it was, it was dank. The dankest, wettest, foulest thing that I have ever smelled in my life. But we were guests, so I didn't say anything. It was clear from Paul's face, and from Stevie's, that they could smell it too. None of us said anything. We just followed him down as he turned on the one bare bulb that illuminated the old cellar.

We stepped down onto the concrete floor, and I heard a bit of a splash. "Sir," I said, "I think that your cellar's flooding."

Rick laughed a little. "No," he said. "Nothing like that. It's just damp, a little bit of moisture." A beat, he swallowed and smiled. "He likes it that way."

A pause. None of us got it, so Stevie asked. "He? Who's he?" A cold, hoarse laughter was the only answer we received. We turned, and I realized something was standing in the corner. A dark form. I knew in a moment that it was the thing we had hit. It looked like a shadow, only a few inches out of the wall, and it glared at us with glowing, intense eyes. Bright red. Small, shining lights in the darkness of its form. If there had been more light, I'm sure that I would have seen all of it, but I couldn't. The thing remained in the darkness, almost like it was afraid of the light. I thank God, now, that I never got a good look at the thing. It's the only way I will ever be able to sleep again. I'm very sure of that.

Stevie started to scream, but Rick wrapped a hand around his neck.

"Please," the thing said in a gravely whisper. "Please, don't scream. I only mean to take what I need. I am a guest in this home, and very grateful. I never take things for myself, never without permission. I eat when I am fed. So, I must ask now, do I have permission, Rick?"

"As always," Rick said. "Of course you do."

I could barely even register what happened next. The dark thing reached out, like the shadow was stretching, and it *pulled* Stevie back into the shadows with it. I got a glimpse of the side of the thing's face when it turned to dig its teeth into Stevie's throat. Its skin was white, sallow. Dry. I tried not to look any more than that. Stevie's screams were more than enough.

I tried to back up, but Rick stood in the way. The thing turned to me, burning into me with its red eyes. "You..." it said. "Don't go anywhere. You're next."

That did it. My mind went on auto-pilot and I fought back. I pushed Rick out of the way and ran upstairs. I slammed the door behind me, grabbing the nearest chair and jamming the doorway. Rick pounded against it from the other side. I didn't listen. I ran for the door.

"Wait!" Edna Mae said, stepping toward me. "Don't run. Don't you understand? It's not our fault. He lived here before we did, but he remains grateful to us as long as we keep him fed. He lures them to us, but we feed them to him. You and your friends are only a meal."

My eyes shifted to the doorway. The woman's insanity hadn't been clear when she opened the door for us, not remotely. But now all the cards were on the table and her mask had slipped away. I thought about making a move for it, but even though the thing was still downstairs and it was only me and Edna Mae, I was terrified. This thing had my friends. People I had loved for years. I never connected with anyone like I did with them and I knew I never would. They needed me.

I had to help them. But I was so, so scared. God, I hadn't even made it to college yet. I didn't want to die.

My eyes turned back to the old woman. Her eyes were big and dark and hollow. The cataract in her right eye seemed to glimmer coldly, like a patch of ice over a dark road.

"Why run?" she said. "What meaning do your lives have out there? You stay here, and you could be legend. Better even, urban legend. Why bother running? Stay here, and he can give you things you never imagined."

I ran through the doorway, back to the car, and I drove until I ran out of gas.

***

I have lived with this memory for ten years now. I went on to college, but I never had a normal life, not after that. Nor a happy one. Something happened that I could not explain. There was a family with a thing in the basement, and they fed the thing to keep themselves alive, and that's as much of an explanation as I will ever need. As I will ever be able to stand. What I do know is that I left my friends to die that night. There's no way around that. We always talked about having each other's backs, but when it came down to it… when they truly needed me I left them there, and I ran, and I didn't even look back. I have lived with the memory, as best as I could. It has haunted me for a very long time.

That's why I'm going back. You see, there have been some reports over the past couple years. Nobody takes them very seriously, just "ghost talk," but some people still insist they've seen something on that road. Sightings of a "white lady" spotted from time to time on Rosemary Way. Sort of a local urban legend. People believe she is trying to lure men to their deaths. Most think, those that believe anyway, that she is just a spirit. But I know the truth. I know that I have been given a second chance. I am starting to think for the first time that maybe I made the right choice after all. Back on Rosemary Way, back just beyond the fork in the road, I think my Sophie is still alive.

And now I am going to get the chance to be with her again. I am returning to the lake, to the road, even to the house if I have to. And when I get there, I will make the choice. I know exactly what the road will be, and how far I will go. In life, everything comes down to the choices we make. It has always been true; it always will be. This choice was made a long time ago.

It's time to see it to the end.

The End.

# The Infant's Fingers

## Erik Hofstatter

Physician: Dr. Edgar
9828-SJE41

The girl's tall shape made it awkward for her to get comfortable in the small bathtub. Hot currents of water rushed through the tap, landing burning drops on her frail knees. The steam devoured the bathroom's frameless mirror, while Diane Blackburn concentrated on her mother's tender touch and thoughtfully considered the assignment she laid before her. Killing someone was no easy task.

"Your life will never be the same after this," her mother sighed, "but nonetheless it must be done. You alone possess the ability to make this plan a success. You are the key. He must die for what he has done to me." Luna Blackburn conspired in a commanding voice full of spite.

Her long and nimble fingers massaged her twelve-year-old daughter's wet scalp. She poured camomile shampoo onto her palms and compassionately stroked Diane's albino curls. The girl gazed into nothingness; her eyes robbed of sight since infancy.

Why was Luna so sure this man deserved to die? "*I must trust in my mother's judgment. She's right, only I alone can do this,*" she reasoned. Diane always knew of her uniqueness. The day she was taken out of public school and isolated from the world, suggested that something must have been amiss. Sometimes, she found the isolation unbearable.

It was no secret that Luna was part of a deeply religious sect, along with her brother, Scott, their position of high importance. Diane's father remained a mystery.

The teenage girl's only knowledge laid in the fact that he left her mother in the pouring rain with a screaming baby in her arms. She dreamed of a day, when she would be reunited with her father. To look into his eyes and ask why he abandoned her all those years ago. Was it because she was different?

Shutting her sightless eyes for a second, Diane tilted her head back and felt the hot water wash away the dirt along with her thoughts. Luna patiently awaited her daughter's response, comforted in the knowledge, that Diane had no other choice but to agree. She wouldn't dare disobey her mother.

Diane swallowed and delivered the verdict in an icy tone: "Alright. Consider your wish fulfilled, Mother. The day after tomorrow, I will use my gift and he will cease to exist." Luna clasped her daughter's albino head with relief and lovingly kissed her forehead.

Meanwhile, inside the hectic Rochester City Hospital, in the far corner of the maternity ward, Dr. Renee inspected the woman that lay on the examination table and softly pressed on her heavily pregnant stomach.

"Well Cynthia, you are ready to burst! My estimation is you will give birth to your daughter either tomorrow night or the night after. How are you feeling?"

The pregnant woman frowned. "Oh, I'm absolutely marvellous," The Doctor grinned; she was used to sarcastic remarks from

women who were ready to go into labour.

"Have you already decided on the baby's name?"

Cynthia buttoned herself up and pushed upright on the bed with some difficulty. "No, but we have a few in mind. My husband, James, should be here any minute so we'll probably make a final decision then." The Doctor smiled and left the room just as James marched in with a bucket of lilies.

"Hey hon, how are you feeling?" he asked and handed Cynthia the delicate flowers. She sniffed them and produced a loving smile. "Ask me anything but that. I get asked that stupid question thirty

times a day by that annoying doctor." Cynthia complained, her voice betraying her exhaustion. James kissed his wife's cheek and playfully caressed her raven hair. He loved her hair.

"Have you made a final decision on the name of our future daughter yet?" he asked. Cynthia glanced into his hazel eyes and sighed: "I think our first choice was the right one. We'll call her Lucy, after your mum." James leaned forward and kissed her forehead. "Lucy it is."

Above the Blackburn residence, dark clouds gathered. The autumn breeze swished through the trees and inside the highest room of the building. Luna Blackburn was putting on her ceremonial scarlet robe. She examined herself in the mirror, noticing that her once shapely form had warped into a skeletal looking creature. Her brother, Scott, sat in the antique Chesterfield chair, his long legs crossed and the same coloured robe covered his body.

A freshly trimmed beard dominated most of his features, his dark eyes closely watching Luna. Scott lifted a glass of Scotch, sniffed it and took a sip. He savoured the taste on his tongue for a few seconds before swallowing. Fingering the glass, he lifted his magnetic eyes to meet his sister's.

"Are you sure you want to go through with this? The girl is innocent," he stated in a pleading voice, "this process is irreversible. You want to sacrifice your own daughter for petty vengeance? The past is past. You cannot change it. Diane doesn't deserve this fate. I beg you to reconsider." Scott delivered his opinion nervously and took another sip of Scotch to calm his nerves. He perceived what was expected of him tonight, yet he needed plenty of encouragement to fulfil his duty. The whisky provided a perfect solution to that problem.

Luna opened an engraved wooden box and removed a curiously shaped medallion before taking a seat opposite her brother. She searched his eyes. He seemed anxious. *"Will he have what it takes, when the time comes,* "she wondered, *"he better or he will pay with his life."*

Scott gazed at his sister intensely, she was calculating something. He knew that look. He could tell by the way she nibbled on her lower lip.

He unlocked his tongue to speak again, but Luna raised her hand to silence him. "I've considered your words, Scott, believe me your opinion matters to me the most. You know damn well I hardly ever heed the words of the other disciples, "she raised herself from the chair and started pacing the room, "you are my brother and I love you, but this has to be done. I know you raised Diane as your own daughter and what you must do tonight will test your devotion to me and this group beyond anything, I asked of you in the past. I planned this day for twelve years. Ever since he broke my heart and left me for that harlot. She could never love him as much as I could. And now I hear she's ready to give birth to his brat. Oh, how long I've waited. No, he must pay. He will pay. If I can't have him, no one will. Come my brother, all is prepared."

She crossed over to him, offering her hand. He accepted and slowly they descended the stairs together, then another set and another, until they found themselves deep in the residence's darkly lit cellar.

Freshly emblazed torches decorated the stained walls while a circle made of sand laid in the middle of the cellar. Foreign symbols were drawn into the circle and a six, black robed and caped figures took their positions around the sacred ground. Scott pulled over his own cape and stepped among the other followers. Luna rose from behind the altar. Candles illuminated her transfixed face.

She opened a tattered book on the altar and raised her hands towards the heavens, before crying out: "MY CHILDREN!! YOU ARE EXTREMELLY PRIVILIGED, FOR TONIGHT, YOU SHALL WITNESS THE SPECTACLE, THAT HASN'T BEEN WITNESSED IN 122 YEARS! WITH YOUR DEVOTION AND ASSISTANCE, YOU WILL ALL SEE THE REBIRTH OF THE GODDESS!"

Luna lowered her hands and sipped from the antique chalice. She swallowed the sweet nectar and wiped her mouth. "SHALL WE BEGIN?"

The six hooded disciples began chanting. She circled every single one and placed the secret mark upon them. "COME FORTH, MY DAUGHTER!" she cried out suddenly and out of the darkness, Diane appeared fully nude. She walked slowly towards the circle, her face blank. Curly, albino pubes covered her genitalia. Her pink skin glowed in the light of the fire. Luna guided her blind daughter inside the circle, bathing her in an unknown liquid. The chanting got louder as the disciples swayed in the rhythm of the chant.

The protesting wind slipped through the cracks and a wave of dust covered the air as Luna retook her position behind the altar.

Diane remained immobile. Her dead eyes fixed upon the blackness, the shiny liquid dripping from her albino hair onto her face. The scarlet robed Scott removed a torch from the nearest wall and approached the girl.

She recognized his repulsive aftershave. *"The metamorphosis will begin shortly, I must accept my destiny, yet why am I so nervous?"* she thought and trembled. The rhythm of the chanting increased while Luna muttered words in a language Diane could not understand. She turned her blind eyes towards the direction of her mother's voice, a glint of doubt spread across her face, but at that moment

Luna cried:" NOW!"

Scott hesitated for a split second but nonetheless obeyed the command of his leader. He thrust the torch towards Diane and the girl ignited in an instant.

Several disciples gasped while the young girl burned like a condemned witch at a stake. Not a single scream escaped Diane's lips.

The girl tilted her head back proudly and raised her arms to the side, as if embracing the flames. Luna's eyes burned with fascination, while her daughter burned truly. She anxiously awaited the final result of the metamorphosis.

The cruel flames devoured Diane's tender flesh and her defeated frame collapsed. Soon, only a smoking pile of ash could be seen where the teenage girl stood and perished.

Scott stepped closer to the bundle of ashes to examine the aftermath. He poked the pile uncertainly with his foot and gasped, when a tiny head of an infant girl emerged from the ashes. He lifted the baby in his arms and inspected it thoroughly.

He could tell it was his niece right away, her teenage mind transported into an infant's body. The baby did not cry, instead it gazed into the man's eyes with abnormal intelligence.

"Diane?" Scott asked in a trembling voice. He has never witnessed anything quite like this before. This resembled the mythical rebirth of the Phoenix. Scott remembered reading about it when he was a boy. *"Is this what happened to her?"* he asked himself in disbelief.

The baby girl nodded, as if sensing his thoughts and the corner of her miniature mouth twitched into a wicked grin.

He covered the baby in a cotton blanket and walked over to the hooded followers. One of them stepped forward and removed the cape. Scott placed the baby in her arms and ordered in a strict voice: "You know what to do."

The woman bowed in acknowledgement and walked out of the cellar. It was Dr. Renee...

Cynthia blissfully slept in the hospital room, participating in the deepest sleep she had in nine months. The birth was a complete success.

James sat devotedly by his sleeping wife and admired her loveliness, even though she just went through one of the most dramatic experiences of her life. She was still beautiful even now in her late thirties, when she was a new mum and James didn't want to admit it, but looked absolutely drained from the process. He inspected her delicate features.

A sudden strain clouded his face, like a painful memory. Dr. Renee walked in and disturbed his train of thought. She possessed a gift for bad timing.

She offered James a warm smile and asked: "How are you feeling?"

He smirked in amusement, remembering his wife's annoyance with that particular question. "I'm fine, thank you. How is Lucy doing?"

Dr. Renee reassured him that little Lucy was doing just fine. "Tell you what, Cynthia should awake any moment, how about I go and get Lucy for you so you can be together for the first time as a family?" She offered and left the room once more.

When her foot crossed the threshold, the smile vanished. Doctor Renee walked down the bright corridor and into the newborn room. Inside, the hectic noise of baby cries made her sick. Spending most her career delivering these things and welcoming them into the world, she now despised every single one of them and never wanted one of her own.

Dr. Renee strolled among the rows of newborns. All of them were asleep or crying, except one. This baby possessed an unusually penetrating gaze and an unmistakeable intelligence lurked behind those grey eyes.

She double checked if no one was looking and tied a nametag around the infant's ankle. It read: LUCY HORN, alongside a six-digit number. Picking the baby in her sturdy arms, she examined its albino hair.

Looking deep into those hypnotic eyes, she commanded: "Do it tonight. Nod twice if you can understand me."

The baby girl studied the woman's mouth for a few seconds as if reading her lips, before meeting her eyes and slowly nodding twice.

"Here we are! Say hello to your new daughter, Lucy." Dr. Renee said delightfully, placing the baby into Cynthia's eager arms. The tiny girl had her eyes closed and looked deep in slumber.

"Isn't she gorgeous?" Cynthia asked, full of pride.

"She certainly gets the good looks from her mum," James complimented and kissed his wife's forehead before kissing his newborn daughter. He played with her small finger and couldn't stop smiling.

*"I'm going to love this little girl more than anything else in this world. If only my other one wasn't such a freak, but Cynthia mustn't now about that. No! I have no other daughter. Lucy is the only one and she is perfect! I will love her with all my heart."*

When he lifted his gaze, the baby's newly opened eyes met his. "Look, she's smiling at you," Cynthia said. Her voice was full of pride and joy. James kissed the baby's slight hand and replied: "Of course she does, she recognizes her daddy."

After two days in the hospital, the little girl called Lucy peacefully slept in her purple decorated room, in the most gorgeous little cot painted with flowers and the rising sun. James lay in his bed, reading one of his favourite historical novels by the mercer lamp.

*"Such a shame Cynthia had to work late tonight. I cannot believe she didn't take any time off after the birth. Is her career more important than her health? Evidently it is,"* he frowned.

He was nervous being alone with his new infant daughter. *"What if something goes wrong? Am I capable of handling an emergency if it presents itself? It's not like I have any choice anyway,"* he thought bitterly.

James put down the book and rolled the silk covers to one side, silently tiptoeing to check upon Lucy for the twelfth time. The baby was asleep. James tiptoed back to his bed and switched off the lamp. The night was hot; he felt little blobs of perspiration forming on his forehead. Rolling onto his right side, he tried to sleep.

When his eyes closed, another pair opened. With adult like agility, the baby climbed down the cot and sneaked towards the kitchen. The moon shone through the window whilst the new-born infant walked unnaturally on her two legs like a fully evolved adult.

Her tiny steps pushed a chair to the sink and she picked up a large kitchen knife with both hands, her miniature fingers struggling to hold the weapon. After a few seconds, she settled for a smaller one.

The infant knew the exact location of the bedroom. Sneaking on the short bed, she inspected the man that snored before her. The task was almost finished.

*"Mother will be so proud!"* The baby thought. She shimmied closer to the man's head, placing the cold blade on his throat. James snored deeply and licked his lips.

The infant hesitated. Suddenly, the man's eyes flew open but it was too late. In that instant, the baby girl slashed to the right with all her might. The knife was sharp. James felt the sudden pain as his artery was sliced open and immediately gasped for breath. The cut was deep, mortally deep.

He felt the warm blood pouring down his body and on the sheets. His life force faded fast as he tried calling for help, but no words escaped his lips.

He gazed into the eyes of the infant, who kneeled on his chest, her grimace triumphant. James looked at her with more intensity than ever before. Only then, in his last seconds of life, he recognized something in that malicious stare.

Lifting his trembling hand with final strength, he reached towards the baby's face and caressed her chubby cheek. "Diane...?" he gurgled, but then his tongue failed him. The infant's shock and horror echoed on her little face.

Her mother's deception finally settled in as she placed her delicate fingers on James's dead face. "Daddy...?" The little girl called Lucy whispered. Then, she began to cry.

The End.

# In Spirit

## William Rasmussen

Physician: Dr. Lotherton
8715-AED19

She's with me now. I can smell her perfume, feel her presence.  God, I wish this had never happened! Even with all the luck I've had, all the money I've won--it's just not worth it. I'd give up this whole world in an instant to see her again, to have her back…

Nikki loved to play the slots. We would drive south from our home in Cordova, TN, to Tunica, MS---some sixty miles or so---at least once a month, just so she could hit the casinos and play the "one-armed bandits." She absolutely loved the sights, sounds and even the smells of the casinos: the wildly original and brightly-colored machines that never failed to seduce her with their improbable payoffs; the monotonous drone of the dinging slot machines, undercut by the elevator-like rock music seeping throughout each establishment; and the oft-times odious aroma of cigar and cigarette smoke perpetually bathing everyone and everything. To say that she was addicted would be understatement. But I loved her, and would do anything in my power to please her.

We had been married for three years. Nikki was twenty-eight while I was a year older. We were still young, career-oriented and untethered by children, so why shouldn't we enjoy a weekend or two gambling every month? I was an up-and-coming accountant with a mid-level firm in Memphis, and Nikki was an assistant manager for a reputable marketing outfit also based in the "Bluff City." Our combined salaries allowed for a hefty disposable income, and even if we lost most of the time, on those rare occasions when Nikki had Lady Luck shine down on her, she oftentimes more than made up for our losses with a single pull of the lever. I had no reason to complain.

The last time we trekked down to Tunica together, about three months ago, we stayed at Resorts Casino and Hotel, where our room as usual was comp'd. Since we played so frequently at any one of a half-dozen casinos rubbing shoulders with the Mississippi River, the hotels connected with those casinos regularly sent us complimentary rooms for a night or two each month in an effort to lure us back. And of course, like carnival marks, we willingly complied.

That Friday evening, we checked in around 7:30, after leaving directly from work with our overnight bags. Nikki and I went straight to our room to drop off our things, before hustling back down to the glitz and glamour of the casino.

"You wanna start with TOP DOLLAR?" Nikki asked as we entered and met a wall of noise. The refrigerator-like temperature dusted my arms with goose bumps.

"Why not?" I said with a smile. "It's your favorite."

She returned my smile, and we made our way over to the fifty cent slot machines.

"Let's try this one," Nikki said, claiming a seat at her favorite TOP DOLLAR machine. I dropped into the seat next to her, and the game was on.

She inserted her Resorts card and fed a "C" note into the machine. We got our two hundred credits and her eyes lit up. She really was a beautiful woman, I thought, staring at her. A trim five-three in bare feet, with short, pixie-ish blonde hair and sparkling blue eyes, she looked stunning in the Technicolor environment. And when her perfume of choice, J'adore, washed over me like a tidal wave, I realized how lucky I was that she'd agreed to be my wife.

She pushed the Credit Button twice to bet a buck, then grasped the lever and pulled. The three wheels spun for a moment, but only one of them stopped on the Pay Line: a triple bar design. "Your turn," she said.

I also pushed the Credit Button twice; but in lieu of pulling the lever, I punched the Spin Wheels button. Two 7's lined up. Still nothing. We continued awhile in this fashion---our gambling ritual---the two of us taking turns, with Nikki tugging on the "one-armed bandit" lever, while I pushed the Spin Wheels button. But after twenty minutes and only a handful of payoffs, she cashed out what little was left of our hundred dollars and we went hunting for another machine.

"How about this one?" she said, pausing in front of a fifty cent WHEEL OF FORTUNE.

"Sure."

We took up seats at this machine and fared better, recovering our initial stake and winning almost fifty dollars before I suggested we grab a bite to eat. You would have thought I was pulling teeth with the effort it took to convince her to take a break. Reluctantly, she agreed.

"Geez, hon," I said when we were seated at a table near the buffet, our plates full, "you really are hardcore when it comes to gambling."

"I just love the excitement and the whole atmosphere, Connor," she said, eyes aglow. "You should know that by now."

I laughed and pushed a forkful of food into my mouth. "I swear, after you die you aren't going to Heaven. You're gonna come back here as a ghost and haunt this place, you love it so much."

"Don't laugh," she replied. "I just might." She reached for my hand and squeezed it gently, winking at me.

We finished our meals and spent the next couple hours roaming the casino like nomads, nesting in front of one machine for a few minutes before moving on to another one, hoping for better luck. When we finally called it quits around 11:30 that night, we were actually up around two hundred dollars. Each of us grabbed a drink of our own "poison" to nurse as we made our way back to the room.

Nikki and I slept in late that Saturday, then we lounged around in bed for a while, talking, watching TV and, lastly, making love. After showering, shaving and finishing our other morning rituals, we scrambled over to a fast-food restaurant within the casino and grabbed lunch. Appetites satisfied, we then wound our way back to our SUV and drove directly across the street to Sam's Town, a western-themed casino.

We spent a few hours there, reacquainting ourselves with the various slot machines and remembering, after dropping our winnings from the night before, that we rarely won at that establishment (Nikki kept a mental inventory of each casino in Tunica, noting, of course, the ones where we had the best fortune).

Climbing back into our SUV, we returned to the Resorts parking lot, where we ditched the car and strolled over to Hollywood Casino. Hollywood was loosely attached to Resorts by way of a covered walkway, but under wholly different management.

After entering the casino, we took a few moments to gaze in wonder at the wide assortment of Hollywood artifacts and memorabilia hanging from the ceiling and clinging to the walls within the set-like interior before blanketing the area ourselves, searching for any slot machine that caught my wife's eye. And for two long hours we simply went through the motions, feeding money into the slots and receiving little in return. Around 5:00 I rescued us from further monetary damage by dragging Nikki back to Resorts for dinner.

"Geez, that was frustrating," I said, sitting at a table in the casino buffet, which we were frequenting once again. "We're down almost five hundred dollars!"

"I know..." Nikki said, a guilty smile playing at her features. "Sometimes I just can't stop, though."

"You know you're addicted," I said, a disgusted look losing battle to a grin on my face. "Sometimes I think you love gambling more than you love me."

"No way!" She reached across the table and clutched at my hand like a starving beggar. "I love you way more, honey. It's just that I love playing the slots, too."

"Right," I said, kidding her.

We lingered over our dinner, enjoying the tasty offerings and making the most of some down time from the noise and the frenzy of the casino. Forty-five minutes later we regrouped and returned to the gambling area a floor below.

Nikki decided to try TOP DOLLAR again, in an effort to turn her luck around. We commenced our gambling ritual, taking turns pulling the bandit's arm then pushing the Spin button. An hour later we still had not made any dent in our considerable debt. I decided to take a break from the action, wandering off for a change of scenery; but not before I covertly watched my wife continue our silly little ritual, alternately pulling the lever for her turn and then pushing the Spin button, as if I were there.

When I returned twenty minutes later, she was ecstatic.

"I'm up over five hundred dollars!" she cried. "I've been hitting everything, honey! Go away again! You're going to ruin my luck." She playfully pushed me off.

Laughing, I backed away and told her I was going to our room for a while to read and watch TV. As I walked off, I stared at her profile for a moment, etching her rapt form in my mind. I didn't realize it would be the last time I'd ever see her alive.

When the local news came on at 10:00 and Nikki still had not come back to our room, I put my book aside, a tiny sliver of concern irritating my stomach. I knew she could become so engrossed in her games that the time would be the last thing on her mind. But it didn't stop me from worrying about her.

I quickly made my way down to the first floor and over to the TOP DOLLAR machine she had last been playing. But she wasn't there, another gambler having taken her place. I cast my gaze around the immediate area, hoping to spot her nearby. No such luck. Pulse quickening, I pulled out my cell phone as I began to canvass the entire floor.

I punched in her cell number, but couldn't get anything at all: no ringing, no voice mail message, nothing. It was weird. As I hurried around the expansive establishment, I wondered if the casino's security system contained some sort of blocking device which made phone service difficult and cheating even more so. I had heard about something to that effect before, but had no idea if it was true. And after repeated attempts to reach my wife by cell phone proved fruitless (my texts to her going unanswered as well), and my search of the gambling premises fared no better, that sliver of concern inside of me swelled to a shard. I felt sick to my stomach with worry. Nikki had never done anything like this before.

But then, I thought, what if I had just missed her on my way down here in the elevator, and she had simply gone up to the room looking for me? Practically holding my breath, I hustled back up to our room, hoping I had guessed right. But I was wrong.

Calming myself, believing there was a very practical reason for her absence, I again rushed down to the casino floor and made another circuit without locating my wife. Then I stopped at every Women's Room on the floor, kindly asking ladies entering the restrooms if they could call out for my missing wife inside. Again, to no avail. I tried her cell again with no luck.

It was now 11:15 and I was scared. I had been looking for her for over an hour now. Myriad scenarios flickered through my mind like a movie reel out-of-alignment. Could she have met a friend and gone somewhere? Could she have simply gone out to the car to get something? Could she have been abducted…? There, I had thought about it.

Nikki was not a big drinker, so I knew that she would have had her wits about her if she had been approached by a stranger. But why wasn't her phone working? It just didn't make sense! And for the first time in almost an hour-and-a-half, as an ice-cold knife of fear carved up my tossing stomach, I considered the possibility that something unusual and horrible had happened to her.

Resignedly, I corralled the first security guard I laid eyes upon and explained the situation to him. He barked something into his handy-talkie, instructed me to wait there, and hustled off. A few minutes later he returned with a supervisor, and I was forced to repeat my story. The two men conferred quietly for a moment before the supervisor escorted me to a small interview room on the second floor.

Captain Jeffers formally introduced himself, then spent the next twenty minutes or so obtaining basic background information from me as well as a description of Nikki and her particulars. With shaking hands, I provided a recent photo of her from my wallet and he promised to return it. He also said his staff was making regular P.A. announcements throughout the casino in an attempt to locate my wife. Then he left the room for a moment before re-entering and informing me that the Tunica Police Department had been notified. We chatted for another twenty minutes or more about my relationship with my wife, our jobs, our habits, our enemies (?), whether we had any children, and other seemingly mundane matters. He also explained that most cell phones now were unaffected by any blocking devices used by the casinos. As my brows furrowed in confusion, another security guard knocked on the door and poked his head into the room.

Jeffers and his subordinate huddled just outside the door for a moment, then he called me over to have a look at something.

Hot sweat trickling down my forehead, my body wracked by nervous, chilly shudders, I followed him like a lapdog, down the corridor to another door that opened into a huge, complex labyrinth of computers, electrical equipment, and overhead TV screens, all of which were overseen by close to a dozen employees. We took seats at a vacant computer monitor, and he played with the keyboard for a while, before directing my attention toward one of the overhead TVs.

"Mr. Neeson," Jeffers said, "is that your wife on the screen?"

I stared at the smallish, flat-screen TV above me, craning my neck to get a better look at the slightly grainy image frozen in time. Sure enough, it was Nikki, most likely at the TOP DOLLAR machine I had last seen her playing. "Uhh…yes, it is. Yeah, I'm sure of it." I was excited now.

"Look closely at the time; our video cameras captured her at this machine for a while, and now it's 9:31 PM. Watch carefully," he said, punching a key on the keyboard, allowing the video to advance in real-time.

I stared at the TV, my eyes glued to the screen, as the video showing my wife, happy, smiling, tugging on the bandit's arm, unspooled for about a minute. Suddenly, Nikki vanished, disappeared, as if she had never even been there.

"What the hell happened?" I said. "Where did she go?"

"We don't really know, Mr. Neeson. I wouldn't worry, though. My men have studied it a bit, and they believe it's merely a glitch in the system." He paused. "But, at least we have a time frame from which to gauge how long she's been gone." He glanced at his watch. "It's 12:30 now, so we can reliably conclude that sometime between 9:32 PM and, say…10:05 PM, or so, when you got there, your wife left the casino. And she's been missing now for about three hours, tops. It gives us something to work with."

Stunned, I asked the man to replay the video clip. I watched it very carefully a second time, and then a third time. Seeing Nikki disappear like that, over and over again, caused a memory of one of our conversations from our first night at the casino to resurface. I recalled our words with morbid fascination…

"…swear, after you die, you aren't going to Heaven. You're gonna come back here as a ghost and haunt this place…"

"Don't laugh…I just might…"

Jeezus, I thought, feeling as if I were in the middle of a Twilight Zone episode. Shudders rippled through my body like earthquake tremors. Unbeknownst to me, tears slowly crawled down my cheeks.

"…a box of tissues, Mr. Neeson," Jeffers was saying softly. "We're going to do everything we can to find your wife, I promise you that."

But even as I reached for a tissue, I knew with unerring certainty that they would never find Nikki. As impossible and preposterous as it sounded, the only plausible explanation that I could hang my hat on would be the implication carried by my wife's unwittingly prophetic words. What else could I consider? Logically, nothing made sense; and yet the only thing that could make sense of this situation was completely illogical. But who would believe me? Dear God, what was I to do?

For the time being, I was transferred back to the interview room, where I waited in silence for a detective from the Tunica Police Department to arrive. I felt as though a huge burden had fallen across my back, the physical sense of loss and my completely otherworldly solution pressing down on me as if I were Atlas bearing the weight of the world on my own shoulders. My mind was plagued by clueless snippets of our last conversations as I tried to work my way through the bizarre, tangled web of which I was a part.

Once the detective arrived, I repeated virtually everything I had already told Jeffers, and I also turned over the photo of my wife that the Captain had given back to me earlier. The detective advised me that he would file his report but, in all likelihood, no actual investigation would commence for 24 to 48 hours, since there was no evidence of foul play or exigent circumstances. I listened numbly as he assured me they were taking Nikki's disappearance seriously, but in many cases the missing person simply showed up on their own within 24 hours or so.

After he left, the hotel manager paid me a visit, offering his sympathies in the matter and reassuring me that I could remain in he room without charge for as long as necessary while the investigation proceeded. I then went back down to the casino to sweep the floor for a while on the outside chance that Nikki had returned.

As I slowly canvassed the area, moving like a zombie and feeling as detached from my surroundings as if I were living in a dream, a strange feeling crept over me, enveloping me and heightening my senses. She was here! Nikki was definitely in the casino near me! And as the familiar fragrance of J'adore tickled my nose, I realized that though she might not be physically present---a ghost, she had said---her essence was close by.

I continued to make my way around the casino, threading through the multitude of gamblers still roaming the floor at this late hour, trying their hand at the various card or dice games and wearing out the slot machines. But the feeling that Nikki was around never escalated any further. Finally, as the hour approached 3:00 in the morning, I decided to head back up to our---my---room and try to catch a few hours of sleep.

I lay in bed for quite some time as my mind was pummeled by a stream of bizarre and conflicting thoughts and scenarios. But, surprisingly, I finally succumbed to the pull of "The Sandman" around 4:00, and didn't wake until a little after 7:00.

Rubbing sleep out of my eyes, I looked over at Nikki's side of the bed, found it empty and, for the first time in over three years, was blindsided by an intense feeling of loneliness. Like a drone, I dragged myself out of bed, showered and shaved, and reached for my cell phone to make some important calls.

I let my office know what had happened and did the same with Nikki's firm; both outfits were shocked but incredibly supportive, begging me to let them know the instant I heard anything. Then, whispering a prayer and holding my breath, I called our parents, both sets of which lived far out-of-town. It didn't go well, but I completely understood. I told them they need not fly in right now, and that I would keep them informed of the investigation as it progressed. Again, they didn't take it well, but tearfully agreed to abide by my wishes.

Next, I hustled down to the first floor to find Captain Jeffers for an update. Of course, there was no news, and no way I could recount what I had felt by myself late last night in the casino without being whisked away for 72-hour observation.

I wandered around the casino for an hour, feeling curiously like a child abandoned by a loved one. Nikki's presence was conspicuously missing this morning, so I tucked tail and retreated to a McDonald's restaurant within the casino for a quick bite. Purely on a whim, I then made my way over to her favorite TOP DOLLAR machine and inserted a twenty.

Almost instantly I sensed her company, like a moth drawn to the flame. Smiling, I began to alternately push buttons and pull the handle, the Pay Line actually doing what it promised. Within thirty minutes, I had won a couple hundred dollars. Then, as suddenly as she had "appeared," Nikki was gone. I cashed out and tried to locate her again, to no avail.

I spent the rest of the day holed up in my room, for the most part, only sneaking down to the casino to see if Nikki was around. But she wasn't.

The next day, a Tuesday, I was visited by the Tunica Police Department detective who had taken my statement and filed a report. He informed me that they were proceeding with their investigation, and that I was no longer a suspect. He explained that since neither Nikki nor I had any insurance policies on each other, amongst several other factors, they would be concentrating their efforts elsewhere. I was moderately offended, but ultimately pleased that they were actually doing their job.

I won several hundred dollars that day on different slot machines, as long as Nikki was "by my side."

I finally returned home on Wednesday, but I've visited Resorts Casino and Hotel every weekend since to be close to my wife.

It's been three months since Nikki disappeared. I guess she got what she wanted. She loved the slots so much. All I know is I look forward to our weekends together, if this is as close as we'll ever be. I just have to adjust to the circumstances and make the most of our extraordinary situation…

She's been here for a few minutes already. I take a seat in front of her favorite machine, feed in a couple of twenties, and begin our special gambling ritual. I push the Credit Button and hit Spin. Nothing. But when I push the Credit Button again, and place my hand on the bandit's arm, she moves closer, as insubstantial as a breath of air. Now hovering over me---her body pressed hotly against my back, left arm lovingly draped across my shoulders, her tender lips teasing my hair---her soft hand covers my own atop the lever. And as we firmly pull down as one on the bandit's arm, I know that the machine will be lucky again today, and that I am so very lucky that Nikki is really and truly here with me…if only in spirit.

The End.

# Orbs of Conflagration

## Luke Tarzian

Physician: Dr. Lichten
6428-SED41

Lucille sweeps the floor. She knows it is dirty, but she cannot see. The church is dark, yet still she sweeps—the temple of her Goddess must be spotless, pristine and immaculate. Cleanliness is mandatory. Otherwise the Ugly Thing will come again; and Lucille does not want that. She remembers far too well what happened when the Foul One trekked the temple halls just seven months ago; she remembers searing pain—the ire of her Goddess. She recalls the particles of dust and dirt, the mud tracked all around the church; the cobwebs in the corners—the filthy picture floods her mind, and from the darkness of that night just seven months ago, she sees the Ugly Thing rise up and stumble towards her; a construct wrought from grime and shadow, two gleaming yellow eyes, a Cheshire grin stretched wide across what Lucille takes to be its head. It whispers to her, leers with hungry eyes, licks its rotting jagged teeth and flicks its serpent tongue. It staggers closer, reaching out, eager for a taste of maiden flesh.

And then it is gone, enveloped in a burst of light, devoured by the heat. The temple quivers and her Goddess shrieks—how could they be so foolish? How could such loyal priests and priestesses allow such ugliness to desecrate a place as holy as this church? How could they let the darkness in? Cleanliness is mandatory; how could they not have known the demon would return should muck still linger? They had all been warned about the ugly

hour countless times—how could this have happened? Was it carelessness? Stupidity? Or had they all conspired—devised a plan to quit their Goddess and move on to something else?

Three lashes on the back; six more on the torso; two across the cheeks; punishment inflicted; retribution much deserved.

Lucille strokes her fair cheek softly at the memory.

She finishes her sweeping, tucks the broom away inside the closet, and prepares to wash the floor. She walks outside to fetch a bucket and some water. The moon is pale tonight and shyly hides behind the clouds, as though afraid to show its face. Lucille smiles—it is odd to think an object so majestic can exhibit traits so human. She wonders if the moon has ever been on holiday; has there ever been a time when Lovely Moon said, "Nay—master I refuse to shine! No longer shall I sway the tides!"

She laughs. It is a silly thought; she knows this, yet it comforts her, amuses her and quells the loneliness of cleaning all alone. She takes the bucket full of water and steps back inside the church, pushing shut the front door, locking it behind her. Lucille lugs the water to the back end of the room, sets it down, procures a cloth from in her apron, soaks it, and begins to scrub. It is a nasty job, she thinks; it is not fair she must clean all alone; but at the same time, it is necessary. A pristine temple is essential, lest she feel the burning fury of her Goddess yet again.

And so, she scrubs and scratches, rubs and drags, humming to herself, singing to forget the pain of raw and frigid hands.

Lucille puts the washcloth down a moment, wiping clean a line of sweat from off her forehead. She tucks her golden hair behind her ears and sighs. She is tired, but she knows the must continue. It would be easier, she thinks, to see what she is doing if there were some light.

But there is none; the temple is bereft of candles. She must make do with what she has, and that is very little, for the moon still shyly hides behind the clouds, and stars have not been seen for several days.

She scrubs some more; and some more; and some more. She has stopped her humming; now she is locked in thought—Lucien invades her mind. Just twelve more days until she takes his name, until the two of them will lie together, joined so passionately. Only twelve more days until she can look deep into his emerald eyes between each thrust, whisper in his ear how much she truly loves and cherishes her Lucien—

The wind is strong tonight and pulls her from the confines of her mind. The winter gusts roll through the room, causing her to shiver slightly for a moment till the wind evacuates. Lucille listens as the branches of the oak trees rattle underneath the zephyr's sway. It is rather peaceful; and the night is still enough to hear the leaves fall to the ground.

She sighs.

Lucille picks up the cloth, soaks it in the bucket, and resumes her scrubbing. The wind blows once again, wanders back into the room, and slithers up her neck, chilling her. She shivers, rattling her shoulders as the cold breeze whispers in her ear. She shudders; such a horrid thing it is, to feel the wind's tongue in your ear. Away with it!

But the gust will not disperse. Frowning, Lucille stands to go and shut the window; but she finds she cannot move, too paralyzed by fear, for in the corner of the room there stands a shadow, leering at her, gazing hungrily with yellow eyes—the Foul One has returned! But how? It cannot climb in through the windows; they are blessed against the darkness, and the doors are all locked tight. She has rid the walls of cobwebs, swept away the dust, scrubbed away the mud. So how—

A set of grimy footprints; Lucille trembles. How could she have been so careless as to not wipe clean her feet? She shakes her head—it is not possible, she thinks! She still has thirty minutes left to clean, before the ugly hour is upon her! How can this be happening? She has always been precise. She has not forgotten! She does not want her Goddess to punish her again!

No...no—she gasps, looking at the silver clock above the window. It cannot be—the dreadful time is here! But how? She shakes her head; she knows—her mother's words play in her head: "It does not do to dawdle in your dreams when tasks at hand must be fulfilled."

She dawdled far too long inside her thoughts, she knows this now, and fears the repercussions of her carelessness.

The Foul One stands before her now; it reeks of something feculent and dead. Lucille shakes, whimpers as the creature's serpent tongue slides down her cheeks, across her scars. The demon's yellow eyes gaze into her deep blues. It whispers to her, like the wind just minutes prior.

*Such a pretty thing you are; such a lovely girl. Eyes that glisten like the sea beneath the sun...hair as golden as the dawn—*
The tongue snakes slowly round her lips—
*Lips as soft as silk and sweet as honey; how I wish that you were mine.* The Foul One reaches towards her with a mangled hand and trokes her slender arms, her waist, her face....

But Lucille is too afraid, inwardly appalled, and so she takes a few steps back.

*I wish to call you mine. I wish to know your flesh, dear maiden.* Lucille shakes her head; she cannot, she is spoken for; she belongs to Lucien. In two weeks-time, her body will be his; she has saved herself for years. She cries now, silently, and prays, asking for forgiveness and for safety.

But her Goddess does not answer this time.

The Foul One staggers near. *I will know your flesh!*
In an instant it is upon her and she cannot move. It pins her to the floor, staring at her with its yellow eyes, grinning hungrily as filthy shadow hands protrude like spider legs and rip her dress to shreds, slide up her thighs and spread her slender legs. Its thorny member slides into her and she cries, shrieks in pain as she is taken. Blood streams down her legs, hot, thick, and premature; she struggles but she cannot move. The Foul One thrusts repeatedly, recklessly, slamming into her. Lucille wails; she can feel its thickness slithering inside, jagged, ravenous, and vile. Its tongue slides round her face and down her neck, a second sloppy tentacle of violation, licking where it should not lick. It slithers down her chest, between her breasts and back again. The Foul One grins perversely, teeth gleaming in the absent light, as it begins to burst. Lucille shrieks again, convulsing, eyes wide as she too climaxes.

At last, the shadow hands withdraw. The demon pulls its sopping member out. Fluid seeps onto the tarnished floor, dripping from Lucille's defiled entryway. The Foul One stands and bows before her, leering horribly whilst she trembles.

*I have known your virgin flesh, and you are mine forever.*

Then the demon shrieks, and in a flash of searing light is gone. Still crying, bruised, and bleeding, Lucille gazes at the light. She does not want to feel the fury of her Goddess; she does not want to know more pain. She pleads, she prays; but it is all for naught. She is unclean.

"You stupid, foolish girl," the luminescence screams. "Have you not learned from past mistakes? Have you not learned the error of your ways? Did your mother's words not resonate?" The temple quakes; the windows rattle; Lucille sniffles, curled into a bloody ball. "And worse yet—you lay with the filth!"

Lucille struggles with her words, she is weak and thus can barely speak.

"Do not try to fashion an excuse, you wretched thing. You have betrayed your Goddess, sullied my good name; and even more— *enjoyed your sin!*" Lucille shakes her head to no avail. "I saw it in your eyes, you filthy harlot, dirty little whore! I saw the passion and the fire!" The radiance is howling now. *"I SAW THE PLEASURE BURNING IN YOUR EYES!"*

Another flash; Lucille is screaming, clutching blindly at her eyes, her body tensing, growing rigid as she writhes upon the floor.

"Carry it from this night forth, for your enjoyment is your curse. You will be as perilous as your transgressions, and all will soon be subject to your sin."

And then the night is still and dark. Lucille wails, still twisting on the soiled floor, a bloody, violated heap, until fatigue takes hold and she falls silent.

***

The voices murmur, whisper indiscernibly. The room is hazy. Figures stand above her.

*Is she dead, the poor thing?*

*What could have happened?*

*It was the Foul One—I am certain of it. Look at all this filth. Yes...but is she...dead?*

The voices pause.

*I-I do not know. The poor girl, she is not moving....*

Suddenly, they scream, a cacophony of agony. In seconds they are nothing and the room feels hot. The figures melt away—

***

Lucille awakes, pulled from the nightmare by a gust of icy wind. She aches all over; she is in pain, yet she forces herself to sit up. She looks down; the blood that covers nearly all her lower half has blackened and congealed; her wounds have scabbed, her bruises blossomed like a bed of ugly, purple flowers. She sniffles, shivers, looks around the empty church. There is no sunlight pouring through the windows, just a sea of gray, lifeless and morose. The temple floor is filthier than ever, painted with her sin, glazed with ash. The dried-up fluid mocks her openly, as does the empty slit between her slender legs. She has been defiled, spoiled by the darkness. How will she explain this? How will she tell her Lucien?

Fresh tears streaming down her beaten face, Lucille pulls herself into a standing position, staggering three steps to the left before she finds her balance. Her dress lies in a tattered heap beside a bench; she is naked; she feels dirty. Lucille whimpers as she looks around for something to conceal her body with: a curtain, sheet, blanket, towel—anything to cover up her sin until she need make mention of it.

But there is nothing, save the remnants of her dress; and so she wraps the biggest piece around her and departs, stepping out into the chilly day.

***

She walks—stumbles, rather—through the woods for what she thinks are hours. But she is not sure—things of more importance occupy her mind. How could she have been so foolish? How could she have let the Foul One in? How...how could she have laid with it...let it enter her?

57

Lucille begins to cry again; her azure eyes are sunken, encapsulated by two thick black circles. She never meant to let this happen; she never meant to draw the ire of her Goddess. She….

Lucille whimpers. How could *She* have let this happen to her priestess? Why had her Goddess let *this* happen? Why had she not rid the temple of the Foul One as soon as it arrived?

Lucille wails. She feels betrayed, confused, uncertain.

In the distance, she hears voices; she can see the light gray smoke rising from a chimney and she knows that she is nearly home. Careful to maintain her balance, she makes for the village, stepping as quickly as her aching legs allow.

She is nearly there.

She hears a voice, a cry, familiar and comforting.

"L-Lucien!" she calls back weakly.

He is running towards her now, a crowd just right behind him. Someone yells to call the search off. Lucien echoes this request. "Call it off!" he shouts. "Lucille is here!"

She is running towards him, they to her. But something is amiss. Lucien begins to slow, so does the crowd. They grip their chests, their eyes wide, faces contorted in some undisclosed discomfort. Lucille comes to a halt, staring worriedly.

"L-Lucien," she cries, "I-I am here…p-please…."

The tears fall faster, harder. Lucille drops to her knees, wailing; a cascade of sorrow.

Lucien and the crowd around him shriek, their bodies glowing some unsightly orange. They are writhing on the ground, twisting in unbridled agony. Lucille watches helplessly; Lucien looks into her eyes, still screaming louder, louder…louder….

Fire. Towering plumes of fire as the bodies blacken. Lucille shrieks, reaching desperately towards Lucien, but he is gone; emerald eyes engulfed in flames of rage and turned to ash. The others in the crowd share in his end, and soon the village burns entirely. Women, men, and children all step out to see what horrid fate has gripped their town, to see what damaged creature shrieks. But one look at Lucille is all they need to understand the others' fate; for they too soon writhe, blacken, and combust, leaving Lucille all alone, shrieking tearfully as home comes crashing down. Even the trees take notice, for they too burst into flames and moan, their great trunks crumbling and crashing down. The birds no longer chirp their morning songs, for when they set eyes on the poor

girl in the center of the blaze, they know what scorching fate has gripped the town and so they turn to ash.

She truly has a stare that sets the world on fire.

The End.

# Bestselling Horror US

**1** The Remaining: Fractured - *D.J. Molles*

2 Snowbound - *Blake Crouch*

3 The Diabolist (The Dominic Grey Series) - *Layton Green*

4 Haunted House - A Novel of Terror - *Jack Kilborn and J.A. Konrath*

5 The Remaining - *D.J. Molles*

6 The Summoner (The Dominic Grey Series) - *Layton Green*

7 Arisen, Book One - Fortress Britain - *G. James and M. S Fuchs*

8 Apocalypse Z: The Beginning of the End - *M. Loureiro and P. Carmell*

9 The Remaining: Refugees - *D.J. Molles*

10 The Remaining: Aftermath - *D.J. Molles*

Compiled June 1st - June 30th 2013
Amazon.com Kindle Chart

# Bestselling Horror UK

**1** World War Z - *Max Brooks*

2 The Grimm Curse (The Girl In The Red Hoodie) - *Stephen Carpenter*

3 The Pumpkin Man - *John Everson*

4 One Blood - *Qwantu Amaru and Stephanie Casher*

5 The Shuddering - *Ania Ahlborn*

6 The Damned Summer (The Ruin Trilogy) - *Scott Weaver*

7 The Time Travel Megapack - *Edward M. Lerner*

8 The Detective Megapack - *Various Authors*

9 Protecting His Mate ( Lycan Romance ) - *M L BRIERS*

10 The Mating Season (Lycan Romance) - *M L BRIERS*

Compiled June 1st -June 30th 2013
Amazon.co.uk Kindle Chart

Group
Therapy
07.13
We talk horror, Zombie
Evacuations and how it all
began.

*We catch up with Jon Ford to discuss horror, organisation and of course how the Zombie Evacuation Races came about.*

### So how did the idea for ZER come about?

The idea for ZER was the splicing together of two of my common interests. I used to enjoy sport in my younger fitter days. My brother and I used to train regularly, I used to play football with my work team and I actually organized my own little basketball league in Birmingham. Basically, I was terrible at Basketball but loved playing and I felt there was no outlet for people like me, so myself and a like-minded work colleague called Brian created our own league which we ran for about 3 years. I was also interested in doing triathlons (inspired by my housemate at the time) and used to enjoy running now and then.

It all got derailed however in 2006 when I blew the ACL in my leg playing football. I also started a new job in London which had me commuting daily. The combination of these two things meant my fitness suffered and I gained weight.

On a parallel track I've always been a massive Sci Fi and Horror geek. I love everything from Star Trek to The Walking Dead. The last few years especially I've been loving the Zombie zeitgeist. For a horror fan like me that skews more towards the Zombie horror and horror comedy it's been like manna from heaven.

Early last year I ended up watching a few Obstacle Course races and ended up taking part in a couple of Spartan Races myself. However, my level of fitness left a lot to be desired which then led me to think about how really fun events like these could be made more accessible to the general public who, like me, might not be uber-fit. And how could we make them more fun too?

The answer seemed to be to me to create a Zombie themed obstacle course race. Not too tough, but a good intro to the sport and with something a bit different that would be fun, especially to anyone who loves Zombies!

I'd set up and run a little Basketball League previously so how hard could it be to set up a race series? Harder than it looks believe me. But with the help of my partner Jess we forged ahead and last years events were an amazing achievement!

***It was deemed a success last year, has anything new been added?***

The events were an amazing success. We had initially thought if we could get 400 to 500 people to come to the event in Cambridge then we'd be happy. We ended up with 3000. And it became so big we did a second date a couple of weeks later in Pippingford near London which had another 2000.

5000 people and that wasn't including our Zombie volunteers, staff, spectators etc. The scale of how big it became how fast really blew us away in our first year.

To be fair, we always had big ambitions last year, probably bigger than we could realistically cope with to be honest, but they were more based around the spectacle and experience we could give the runners. We then pushed our social media as hard as we could and campaigned in the areas we were holding the events and just tried to get our name out there. We had a fantastic group of Local Promoters that came on board and helped spread the word and we're looking for more this year, so if folks out there are reading this and are interested then let us know!

We did however learn a lot of lessons last year. Our first year was always going to be a steep learning experience and we're changing some things and putting into practice some ideas and contingencies this year which will hopefully make the event even more fun and run in a slicker more efficient way.

There were also things we just couldn't do last year for budgetary reasons. Obstacles we wanted for example. This year we've got plans to do some of them. Some of them are really exciting ideas too. The aim was always to make the event somewhat theatrical in nature so our obstacles and set-pieces are themed around things we've seen in Zombie movies or TV shows. This year we think we've stepped that up to a new level and it should hopefully be lots of fun!

***Do you have a funniest moment that stands out?***

There were a number of awesome moments from last year. Hearing the screams on the course from the big tough grown men never failed to elicit a chuckle. It was great knowing that the rough and tough had come to the event and we'd scared them into screaming like little girls.

There was also some amazing Zombies on the course, including one guy called Simon who was a Zombie clown. He was hilarious and scary at the same time and everyone was talking about him. This year's Zombie volunteers have a lot to live up to. I think Simon is back again this year and has told us he is upping the ante this year. He won't tell us what he's going to be but we're eager to find out.

Looking back with hindsight we also had an amusing moment when our bag drop tent almost blew away in the horrendously windy conditions, honestly the weather was so bad for a while with wind and rain and even a hint of snow. It was panic stations as we tried to get the tent pegged back down. We had volunteers from the crowd come forward to help us hold it down and one of the caterers on site parked his car on the end of the tent to hold it in place. At the time it was one of those "ARGH!!!" moments, but looking back it was hysterical and was a great example of what amazing people our runners were in helping us out.

***What was the general feedback from survivors?***

Really excellent. Better than we could have hoped for or imagined. Everyone seemed to love the event and said they'd be back. We got lots of constructive feedback from the people who had been too, which was really nice. It was a good crowd of people who didn't moan or whinge about. We were always honest about it being our first year and I think it gave us an air of good will from our runners, so rather than moan about things they didn't like they just constructively fed back to us, which was very much appreciated. It gave us great information to use this year to improve things.

Hopefully we'll see lots of returnees this year. We give different medals to the survivors and the infected on the course when they finished last year and the first thing most of the survivors said was "We're coming back next year to get the Infected medal!"

So, while the runners who were infected last year will hopefully be back to try and survive, there will be an odd group of people on the course simply begging the Zombies to take all their lives and infect them!

### *What can new runners expect?*

They should expect a fun filled scary run through various terrain types negotiating various obstacles and set pieces that are themed after their favourite zombie movie moments. It's a 5km course with around 20 obstacles on it, none of which are too hard but make life interesting and challenging when you're being hunted by hordes of ravenous Zombies. And whether you survive the course or are infected there's a prize awaiting you a the finish line.

Come and run as a group for the best time and expect to get tired, dirty, wet, bloody and above all scared! Even if you don't think you can run 5km come and give it a whirl! You'll be amazed at how far you'll run when the adrenaline is pumping and a Zombie is trying to eat your brains!

Everyone seemed to finish the race with a smile, win or lose last year and that is all we wanted from the event.

### If you had the budget what would you add?

If we had an unlimited budget there are so many obstacles we would love to add in. Some of it real pie-in-the-sky stuff. For instance, the Cambridge race on October 5th is in Carver Barracks and there is a runway there. We would have loved to rent a big Army cargo plane for the day and have the finish line be as you run up the boarding ramp ready to be flown to your evacuation destination in a faraway country. You never know one day perhaps. LOL

Realistically though there are loads of obstacles and set-pieces that we've seen in films or TV shows that we want to give our runners the experience of. We have a huge 'bible' of them in the office. As and when we get the money to do them (and do them properly!) we'll put them on the course, so I'm not going to spoil anything by giving away our secrets now!

### What would you like to say to any of your zombie volunteers (past and upcoming)?

To the past ones "THANK YOU" and "PLEASE COME AGAIN!". They really made our event something special last year and we'll always be grateful for that.

To anyone thinking about coming this year, please do. The more the merrier. What would an event set during a Zombie apocalypse be if we couldn't provide a zombie festooned apocalypse? If you have friends or family that love dressing up and

roleplaying as Zombies then this is a chance to come and do it and genuinely scare people. We're not like the Zombie walks etc where you just turn up and walk around town (not that there is anything wrong with that!) but we are probably the only event in the UK where we will accept hundreds of volunteers to come and actually BE Zombies for a day. Zombies with the intent purpose of infecting and devouring our evacuee's.

___

If this sounds like fun to you then get in touch and come along! You can find all the details about being a volunteer Zombie on our website.

***How important would you say social media has been to raising the profile of ZER?***

HUGE! Last year especially we did very little media publicity outside of social media. Basically, we spread the word via Facebook and Twitter and through cross promotional partnerships with likeminded businesses. One of our biggest social media supporters has been a site called Bleading Marvelous which is shop that sells all kinds of horror related merchandise and accessories. We really want to become a well-known event in the Zombie and Horror related community, and hopefully a 'MUST DO' event on their calendars, whether they want to run away from the Zombies or BE the Zombies. With that idea in mind we love networking our way out through these like-minded businesses. We can push their product to our fans and they can push us to theirs.

The results last year were awesome and we had more people at our races than we expected and we're looking to top that this year.

We're also very open and honest on our Facebook page. If someone is posting on Facebook, 9 times out of 10 it's me or Jess, so you have direct access to talking to us. We love to encourage a sense of fun and community where we can and we try and keep everything as transparent as possible. For example, if we have problems with venues or anything, we'll let everyone know about it as soon as it happens, like we did last year when we had to switch from our original venue at Bassingbourn to a site just down the road called Apocalypse Paintball. Our prices are listed on the website and are transparent, there is no hidden service charge or tax hit, we list EXACTLY what the runner can expect to pay.

I think people are more inclined to stick around with a company long term if they feel that that company cares about them sticking around, and hopefully we show that we do care. And personally, I love the direct communication I have with our followers, or 'Zombie Nation' as we call them. You meet such fantastically interesting people.

***With regards to horror you clearly have a love / respect for zombies. When did it begin?***

Way back in the dim and distant past. As my partner would attest to, I love 'B' movies, especially anything Kaiju. Give me a monster movie and I'm a happy man. This started with me watching the 'Saturday Morning Creature Features' in my youth. Godzilla, Mothra, Gamera… love it all. So that's where it starts, but when you start walking on that path it inevitably leads you to related stuff. Before long I was diving deep into the depths of the Troma back catalogue, 'The Toxic Avenger' and things, and then from there in the 80's I discovered the joys of George A Romero and especially his Zombie movies. I'm a traditionalist when it comes to my Zombies. My favourites are the slow shuffling hordes that most people think about when they think 'Zombie'. I enjoy the faster 'rage' zombies too, and did enjoy World War Z recently, but my heart is with those traditional Zombies. They can be uber scary when done right.

I'm loving the fact that we're in a real golden age for Zombie related things at the moment. I'm loving The Walking Dead TV show, as a long-time reader of the books it's great to see something so tonally accurate. The recent TellTale Games game was awesome too. And I also love comedy so despite it probably being clichéd my fav Zombie movie very easily and very quickly became 'Shaun of the Dead'. It's a perfect blend of comedy and horror which honours the source material instead of spoofing it.

***Is your love for just zombies or are you a horror fan in general?***

I'm a general horror fan, but Zombies tap into all the right aspects for me to be my favourites. I love the 'monster' aspect of it. I'd much rather watch a horror film with vampires, werewolves or some other monster than I would something like the 'Saw' series. Zombies are an analogy for our world. I've always thought that the slow-moving shuffling zombies represent an inevitability of something. They are slow and plodding but they are by their nature relentless and it doesn't really matter how fast or far you

run, or how well you try to all yourself in and defend yourself, they're always coming, and eventually they'll get you.

In the recent 'World War Z' movie the zombies are being used for a different analogy. They aren't so much zombies as a physical representation of the spread of a virus or plague. In that way the film has much more in common with films like 'Contagion' or 'Outbreak' than it does with 'Day of the Dead'.

It's this that makes them relatable to me and that makes them more interesting than their horror stable mates like Vampires and Werewolves et al. Zombies aren't monsters in a traditional sense, they have no personal motivation, they are a force of nature almost, and in a lot of respects humans versus nature is the oldest story on the planet. I'm fairly sure that the cavemen of old were supremely worried about zombie Mammoths back in their day. Positive even, I'm sure it's even represented in some cave drawings.

***Is there a part of the horror genre that you hate?***

I find personally that Horror is such a wide genre, where do you draw the line. For example, I'd class 'Shaun of the Dead' as horror, but it's funny and it's not terribly scary. But it treads all the same tropes that my favourite zombie movies of 60's, 70's and 80's that I love. Is something like 'Dexter' a crime show? A horror show?

Hate is a strong word but I don't really have any interest in the 'slasher horror' aspect of the genre (though I love crime stuff, 'Dexter' and the recent 'Hannibal' being highlights in that respect). I have no interest in the likes of 'Human Centipede' et al.

It's not that I hate them, they just don't thrill or excite me in any way. I don't like horror films that only have the intent purpose to shock me, I like something a little deeper, something I can think about or that will move me in a different way. It also needs to be clever and not just a rehash of an old idea with a different protagonist.

One of my favourite recent horror type films is 'Cabin In The Woods'. It epitomizes everything I love in the genre. It's a brilliant film that I don't think enough people have seen and I have no idea why!

***What do you think the next big thing in horror will be?***

I have no idea it would all be guesswork. Horror tends to trend according to what is troubling the word at any given time. Zombies are a reaction to today's reliance on technology and the fact that the world we live in is in danger of turning us into zombies as we are. How many times have you seen a group of people together somewhere and they're ALL on their smartphones rather than talking to each other? I'm as guilty of this as anyone.

'Shaun of the Dead' brilliantly parallels this in its opening credits where we see the drudgery of day to day life superimposed over Zombie apocalypse and wonder if there is really a huge difference. Indeed, it takes Shaun himself in the movie a while to twig that something is going on.

Go back a decade and the cinemas were full of disaster flicks threatening to tear the world apart. This was a world that feared being torn apart by terrorism after what happened in the US on September 11th.

It's inevitable that something new will come along to take the place of Zombies in being horrors next big thing, but I really don't know what. We may need to see what the world throws at us next before we make that jump though. I tend to think we may see some smaller more personal horror movies come down the pipeline driven by the movie industry and their current troubles.

Movies have an issue where we live in a world of downloadable content. People are now streaming whole series of TV shows to watch and in that arena, we can have more story, more character development and more suspense. Movie studios are I think realizing there is a culture shift and as such we're seeing increasingly more and more 'spectacle' films and sequels, and less and less the smaller movies. I think these will jump to TV. TV is getting huge kudos lately with TV shows like Game of Thrones, Breaking Bad, American Horror Story, The Walking Dead and Hannibal getting rave reviews and big names signing up to work on them. I think TV is where the interesting stories will be told now that the shackles of episodic story telling are now off.

I think we could be on the verge of some GREAT horror TV stuff coming down the pipeline. Hope so anyhow. The shows I mentioned above are complicated, dark at times, have amazing production values… Everything I want.

*Do you have a favorite horror author?*

I really don't. I read prolifically when I'm not too busy (life is hectic at the moment) but I tend to flit between genres and authors. Richard Layman was probably my first dabble in horror books, which ironically led me to the likes of Stephen King and

Dean Koontz etc. I read Max Brooks – Zombie Survival Guide and loved it, but am ashamed to say I haven't read 'World War Z' yet (although I have just seen the film so maybe it's just as well I wasn't in anyway swayed by reading the book first!). I'm currently gearing up to read 'The Hanging Tree' which is another Zombie book by the author David Andrew Wright.

I have to split horror book reading time with Sci Fi and Crime time. I do love Jeffrey Deavers books, especially the Lincoln Rhyme books (like The Bone Collector). He's probably the only author I really consistently follow though these days.

*Going back to the ZER, can you take us through the prep before race day?*

The Zombie Evacuation Race takes an awful amount of prep work, but thankfully we have a good team of folks who are veterans at this.

There's so much to do from the booking and scouting of venues, to the logistical planning to the sorting obstacles and things out for the event. And then there's the marketing and advertising and social media and doing interviews like this one.

On race day while the runners turn up an hour before their heat the volunteers are onsite from around 9am, and we're on site from around 6am!
We have to set up the course, the registration area, get our Zombies all ready and on course and briefed... so much to do. And our day doesn't end till we've taken the course down. It's a long day for the ZER staff, but an exciting one.

*Any surprises planned that you can share?*

Hmmmm alas no. I'd love to... but I can't. It's one of those "I could tell you but then I'd have to kill you" kind of deals.

The nature of the event is that we plan to surprise and scare our runners and give them a unique experience with is half obstacle course race and half theatrical zombie survival. We do have surprises on the course, but to tell you what they would be would be to spoil the surprise and we hate spoilers here are ZER.

However, to give you some ideas of what to expect last year we ambushed our runners within yards of the start line giving them something to scream about. We're not going to do that this year as people will expect it, but we do have other ideas up our sleeves to keep it fresh.

So sorry, no spoilers here!
*Will you be running in one / all episodes?*

I will indeed! I'll be running at the Cambridge event. I'm doing it for charity so all my sponsorship proceeds will go to the Make-A-Wish UK Foundation. I'm very much looking forward to it

as although last year I got to organize it, my biggest regret was I didn't 'experience' the race for myself. I'll remedy that this year so I'll see what the runners go through on the day and what they experience.

*You recently showcased ZER at Scarecon, how was that experience?*

Scarecon was a great experience. It's a trade show for the Scare industry and it was a great event for networking and we made so many contacts that could be super helpful to us going forward in all aspects of the industry, from doing FX makeup to cross promotional opportunities. We're always looking for people who can help us and would like to be a part of the Zombie Evacuation Race experience.

*Are you exhibiting at any other conventions before the episodes kick off in October?*

None planned for horror conventions, though we're always up for invites! We are planning to attend a few Comic Conventions over the coming months and we'll be at a few fitness expo's. But nothing firm as yet.

*Thank you for your time Jon, I hope the events go well and you will be running them for many years to come.*

If you are interested in running in one of the ZER's you can find more information in Sanitarium issue 010. Or check out their website:

Main race dates are on the following dates:

EAST ANGLIA - 05/10/13

SCOTLAND - 12/10/13

WEST - 20/10/13

SOUTH - 27/10/13

Modern Grimmoire: Fairy Tales, Fables and Folklore
By Indigo Press
Review by Casey Chaplin


While reading *Modern Grimmoire: Fairy Tales, Fables and Folklore*, I began to think. I didn't think about the works, individual or as a whole, but rather why somebody would choose to purchase an anthology over a novel. Traditionally, the book market is saturated with various genres of novels leaving little room for the short story, or short story collections, however *Modern Grimmoire* could be the one to change that. Yes, it does seem naive that one collection of shorts could sway the population into reading anthologies, but we do have to start somewhere, *Modern Grimmoire: Fairy Tales, Fables and Folklore* offers up so much more than just a collection of short stories.

This anthology keeps reading the multitude of stories interesting by interjecting other bits of literature to keep your mind fresh and enthralled in the pages. Every so often, after finishing a story you're met with a lovely poem. Sure, it may seem a bit out of place, but upon reading it, your mind is settled and ready to read the next story. Not just ready, but eager and excited. However, just having poems break up the chronicles can grow tiresome as well, and so you get artwork strewn about the pages. All of these touches are there for a reason, and as a reader you may not even notice them all that much. But if you find yourself reading *Modern Grimmoire*, do read the poems, and admire the art - they are what make this anthology special.

As nice as the poetry and art happen to be, they aren't what this collection is all about; it's about the stories, and I can say with certainty that the tales told within this book are some of the finest short stories I have read. Each one is interesting in its own way, from first person accounts, to third person narratives, the stories are for the most part gripping and a joy to read. Indigo Ink Press clearly put a lot of thought into what went into this particular collection, and truth be told, it shows. There are countless authors who have contributed to this work, and each have their own style and take on this fantasy genre, and each is skilled at their art.

Of course, not every work within the collection is made of solid gold, but even the lesser stories, the ones I didn't enjoy as much were still very well written and managed to keep my attention until the very end. Alternatively, there were some very entertaining ones as well. Stories that drew me in so completely that I didn't want them to end where they did, but alas, they must for it is indeed an anthology - and like all good things, the stories must come to an end.

I've reviewed a few collections/anthologies in the past, and this one stands out as the best. Even if short stories, poetry, or artwork isn't your fancy, I would still suggest this to you.

## *VERDICT:* *93%*

About Casey Chaplin:

Casey Chaplin is a horror writer, reviewer, and content creator. He has written a full-length horror novel entitled Lizzy; competed several screenplays for production, and writes reviews for various websites and magazines including Gamers Mantra and Sanitarium Magazine. He has an education in Radio Broadcasting, with a major in Creative Writing and has worked both full time and freelance for several radio stations.

NOS4A2
By Joe Hill

William Morrow & Company

Review by Rob Salem

With his third novel, NOS4A2, Joe Hill has struck gold in reimagining the vampire legend and blending it with the fantastic. While not properly a vampire story, NOS4A2 definitely evokes many of vampirism's most terrifying elements and weaves them into a creative new monster in the guise of the story's villain, Charlie Manx, complete with gullible and grotesque henchman, Bing.

The storyline runs over the course of several years, following protagonist Vic 'The Brat' McQueen from her childhood into her adult life, as she uses her two-wheeled rides supernaturally span great distances in search of lost objects. Eventually, Vic learns of Manx and as a child encounters him but manages to escape him. Years later, Manx attacks Vic and takes her son, Wayne, to his between-worlds lair, Christmasland. The story climaxes with a confrontation between Vic and Manx and closes with a short epilogue in which Wayne and his father, Lou, end Manx's curse on them. Of special note to the storyline is Manx's car, The Wraith, which echoes Hill's father's (Stephen King) interest in using vehicles as characters.

Hill has successfully written an engaging story that mixes vampirism, child-predators, and Christmas, while making not so subtle modern popular culture references (the name Charlie Manx evoking Charles Manson, the motorcycle riding heroine Vic McQueen and her son Bruce Wayne, for example...). Manx even pokes fun at this himself when his henchman, Bing, asks about The Wraith's license plate, from which the book takes its title, saying,

"It is one of my little jokes. My first wife once accused me of being a Nosferatu."

Overall, the blend of light humor mixes well with the tension created by Hill's writing style and keeps the reader on the edge of their seat while waiting to see what happens next; it's also a clever means of exposition that lends itself well to the notion of Manx's use of Christmas as a cover for terrible horrors he inflicts upon children (such as with the word-play of 'Sleigh House,' which is both something you'd expect from a campy B horror flick yet terrifyingly sinister when its purpose is considered). Other elements of the story link it to other horror universes, such as those of King and Lovecraft.

NOS4A2 is an excellent entrant into the annals of horror literature and an absolute must-read for fans of Joe Hill or Stephen King that will appeal to fans of classic and modern horror alike.

## VERDICT: 95%

Classics Review:
Carmilla
By J. Sheridan LeFanu
Review by Rob Salem

First published in 1872, the lesser known and much shorter Gothic vampire novella 'Carmilla' by J. Sheridan LeFanu predates Bram Stoker's 'Dracula' by about 25 years, but any comparison of the two tales can readily identify LeFanu's influence on Stoker's work, and all subsequent versions of the classic vampire story.

'Carmilla' tells the tale of the vampire Countess Mircalla Karstein's interaction with the story's narrator, Laura. As a young child, Laura has a dream-like encounter that sets the stage for a meeting with Carmilla twelve years later. Over the course of her narration, Laura tells of how the mysterious Carmilla comes into her life, makes sexual advances on her, and is ultimately revealed as the Countess Karstein before her destruction by General Spielsdorf and Baron Vordenburg.

LeFanu's writing is characteristic of the Gothic style, being eloquent and fluid, with each sentence carefully crafted to perfectly make its point, and it is this style of writing that creates the Victorian atmosphere that is almost a requirement of the classic vampire story. Laden with sexual tension that sets the stage for virtually every lesbian vampire since this work's original publishing, 'Carmilla' is an often-over-looked cornerstone in vampire mythology. Other innovations in LeFanu's work are the introduction of the vampiric love interest (Laura in this story, mirrored in Lucy and Mina in Stoker's story) and the experienced vampire hunter, and through Stoker's versions of these staples of the vampire tale, these figures have become virtual archetypes of the vampire legend.

About Rob Salem:

Rob Salem is a well-traveled poet and writer from Northern Indiana. He is lives in a quiet, rural neighborhood with his wife and son. He spends his weekends participating in historically oriented hobbies, playing guitar, and enjoying good cigars and good beer.

Look out for more reviews in our next issue.

# COMPETITION

WINNER:
Patrick Higgs

From the editors at Writer's Digest, this fantastic resource for horror writers details hundreds of magazine and book publishers who are interested in acquiring and publishing new frightful fiction. Each market listing provides information on where the publisher is located, what they're looking for, who to contact, how to reach them, and what their terms are. Each entry also comes with special insider tips for getting their attention. You want to get your horror fiction published? Start by looking here.

The name of the winner will be printed in next month's issue

Keep on writing and good luck!

Screenplay by Katie Robinson

CLAYTON HILL SANITARIUM

# Breaking Out

## Davinder Johal

Physician: Dr. Peterson
S268-WCT29

Keel was a hard man, tempered by a childhood in high rise city slums, followed by a life of crime, leading to long stint at Her Majesty's pleasure in hill top, fortress like prison, in Armley, West Yorkshire.

Keel didn't worry none when the screws brought in the new prisoner. Lounging on the top bunk he pretended to read the paper, casually turning the pages, and tried not to show the sudden shock that rocked him as the new con moved in.

Abe Steiner was ancient, with skin like cracked leather. His eyes were sunken pits, creased and lidded by an overture of excess flesh. His jaw seemed too big, stretching the skin around his mouth into a lipless smile.

Above all it was the way Abe Steiner moved that really made Keel feel edgy. It was as if Steiner's joints hadn't been made to function together. He looked more gargoyle than man. They probably got him on charge of vagrancy and extreme ugliness, thought Keel.

Steiner immediately began pacing the ten by ten cell, muttering under his breath, like Keel wasn't even there. Steiner's movements were sudden, sharp and awkward, tilting and swaying in mockery of nature.

Keel sighed; they'd put him with another nutter. He determined that whatever mental or physical aberration disturbed Steiner, he wasn't going to allow anything to ripple his own cultivated sense of zen calm. It was all too easy to let this place get to you, some inmates ended up harming themselves, others doled out aggravation to those weaker themselves, but Keel worked at keeping calm, working out his energy in the exercise yard. Only when pushed did Keel show the steel at his core. He'd taken everything prison life could through at him with only two tiny scars to show for it in the last five years. As a result, he got to share the cell with the young, the old, and bent accountants. Now add to that, ugly nutters.

Well a muttering cripple like Steiner wasn't going to worry him none.

But Steiner did irritate him.

'Christ on a crapper', thought Keel, as Steiner paced. Keel tried to strike up a conversation with him, after all he was going to share a cell with the guy. Steiner proved uncommunicative for the rest of the evening. He muttered to himself, seemingly getting more and more agitated. Later, Steiner fidgeted in the bunk below Keels, who fell into a fitful sleep and dreamt of walking across a field of bones that crunched and snapped underfoot.

At reveille next morning, Keel awoke shivering. Steiner was pacing, his constant muttering now punctuated by moans. It didn't look like Steiner had slept at all. It's as if Steiner lived in own world oblivious of all around him. Suddenly Keel felt a keen dislike to the old man. Not because of his obvious age, or his looks (which were bad enough), but because of the way his eyes jittered around in their sockets and the way the guy radiated nervous tension. Keel could feel his carefully nurtured zen calm crumbling in the old man's presence.

Steiner was crazy, after all, someone must have smashed the glass in the tiny cell window last night. Did the crazy bastard think he could escape that way? What about the bars? and, the sheer drop in prisons cliff like walls.

When Keel returned from the rec period, Steiner was silhouetted against a steel sky. His head was pressing into the gap between the bars. Steiner's left-hand gripped a bar twisting back and forth as if he could work it loose. His other hand hung limp at his side. Keel noticed the ugly bruises on Steiner's arm and calming effect of physical exercise started to evaporate.

Steiner looked back over his shoulder, his eyes momentarily ceasing their nervous motion and he focused his attention on Keel.

'The winds picking up, I'm getting out, out of here'. Then his eyes jittered away again and Keel was no longer there for him. Keel heard him mutter.

'Got get out, got to fly out of here. The wind will fly me out'. Keel climbed on his bunk. 'Poor crazy bastard,' he thought, and then, 'sweet Jesus on a donkey, why do I always get them?' He decided he didn't like Steiner much, a guy like him would make it so much harder to do his time, and listening to Steiner muttering and pacing again, the remaining 3 years of his sentence stretched to an eternity. He sighed, it would be all too easy to start hating Steiner, but crazy people usually got that way because they hurt somewhere deep inside, where nobody could or would help. A rare compassion stirred Keel into speaking.

'You better see a doctor about your arm man.'

'Doctor?' Steiner, now back at the bars, stared out as if he could will himself out. 'No! No doctors, I don't trust any white coats.' Steiner was bent like a shallow C, as if the effort of talking had hurt him. Steiner's voice was low, at once hugging the grey painted concrete floor and then rising into the deepening shadows in corners of the cell. The sun had dipped below the horizon. Keel could barely see him. Only Steiner's small bony hand restlessly working at the bar told Keel that he was still there.

'Yeah, there all a bunch of Nazis here man, even the docs.' Keel said, attempting again to make some sort of connection.

'Nazis,' Steiner whispered, 'Nazis', louder. He turned, moving awkwardly to the centre of the cell, his eyes reflecting sharp points of light from those wrinkled black pits.

'Oh shit,' thought Keel, with a name like Abe Steiner, he was probably a Jew. He looked old enough to have lived through the last war.

'Hey look, I'm sorry man.' Keel started.

'Do you know what Hitler's National Socialist,' Steiner spat out the words, 'did to me, do you have any idea.'

Steiner moved into the corrugated beam of twilight that that threw long rectangles of light onto the cell door.

'Look at me,' he hissed, 'look at me!'

Steiner slipped out of his prison regulation shirt and pants. Keel didn't speak, couldn't speak. He didn't want to look, but the alien shadows that filled the hollows of Steiner's body magnetized Keels vision. Suddenly the small cell felt positively claustrophobic. Every shadow stretched like a living thing, as Steiner's body revealed its awful wonder.

Steiner was as wrinkled as an ancient tree, his flesh hanging off him as if his skeleton had shrunk without giving the rest of his body time to respond.

'Christ on a crutch', Keel whispered, Steiner's skeleton didn't just look too small for the flesh that hung off it in thin folds, it looked as if God had played a surreal joke, and made Steiner of odd leftover bones.

Steiner turned under the fading light as if on a revolving platform, his hip bones sliding under his skin like slow pistons. His ribs covered one moment by a fold of flesh then rippling like waves in a pool, the next. His left hand, thin and birdlike clawed at the air to help him turn. Scars circled his joints, reflecting like dull steel with each cast of light on his fantastic flesh. Steiner looked like some alien carcass marked for filleting.

'Do you see now, why no doctors,' he said. 'Doctors did this, Nazi doctors. And doctors, any doctors would do it again if they knew.'

'Knew what?', thought Keel.

'That's why I have to get out. I must break out. God help me, I have to break out, before the doctors come.' Steiner continued murmuring as he tugged on his clothes and lowered himself into the bunk below Keel's.

The night drew on and only dim lights burned in the prison now with the strange hollow cries of prisoners dropping through the dark like pebbles dropped into an empty well.

Keel couldn't sleep. Holy Mary in a miniskirt, what had happened to Steiner? Whatever it was, Steiner had taken out mortgage on the nut-house a long time ago, that was for sure. As midnight approached Steiner was still murmuring restlessly. Keel had almost surrendered to sleep when Steiner moaned. The sound was low, deep and ragged.

Then a dull sound like snapping of wet branches from the bunk below banished all sleep from Keels mind. He tried not make a sound. His own breath seemed to rasp noisily in his chest. For the first time in years of prison life Keel was unnerved. He didn't know what to do, except listen.

Steiner moaned louder. Pain, endured.

Keel's heart began to thud in his chest. Christ in heaven what was he doing?

Steiner seemed to be pleading with himself.

'Got to break out before the doctors come, got to break...'

Sssnap.

That sound was awful, hooking nerves in Keels gut and bowels, so that he felt like vomiting and crapping himself at the same time.

Steiner uttered a low animal sound.

'...these bones, got to break out...break out these bones...', he seemed to be crying desperately.

Sssnap.

The sound seemed to squeeze Keel's brain. An image of himself holding his mother's hand in the butchers, surrounded by moist slabs of meat came to him. He must have been about six or seven. Looking up to the wooden bench where the butcher, a heavy-set man, had been forcing apart the haunches of a pig until the hip joints cracked inside the thick pink flesh. That was the sound Keel heard from below.

Sssnap.

Keel couldn't stand it any longer. He felt panic and madness swelling like boil in head.

'Stop it. Stop it. Steiner, stop it.'

All sound ceased from the lower bunk.

'Jesus, Steiner what the fuck did they do to you man?' He wanted Steiner to talk. Anything to stop those awful sounds. For a while there was nothing, just a bloated, unbearable silence. Then Steiner spoke.

'The Nazi doctors, the devils. You ask me what they did?' 'They broke my bones; again, and again.'

'We were just laboratory rats to them, to do with as they pleased. To die or suffer as they wished. In the last years of the war the Nazis were getting desperate. What with that madman leading them, and Himmler still dreaming of a master race, they dared any atrocity for their cause.' Steiner paused, sucking in wheezing ragged breath.

'They wanted supermen who could suffer horrific injury and still recover. Men who could die for the fatherland, again and again,

'For this aim they sacrificed us, in the name of their godless science.'

'They made monsters.' Steiner's voice was hoarse.

'A long time ago, before the Nazis took me, I was tall. I stood straight and proud. I was even handsome. Can you believe that now? But for my dark eyes and hair I could have been one them,' Steiner said bitterly.

'I was like you with good strong bones. That's why they chose me, for my bones..'

Steiner's speech became inaudible for a while and then lapsed into silence. When he continued, the anger and bitterness seemed to have drained away, lanced like an ugly boil by his previous outburst. Now Keel heard the voice of a broken survivor.

'You've got good bones Keel. Don't let them take your bones, it's hard to get good bones.' Steiner trailed off again, sobbing quietly. An old man who had been through hell.

Sleep came uneasily to Keel that night. Steiner's crazed whispers echoed in his dreams.

'You've got good bones Keel.'

'It's hard to get good bones.'

'They made monsters, monsters who break bones.'

Keel woke suddenly. Cold stung his bare back and he began to pull up the blanket when movement caught his eye. There in the middle of the cell, Steiner huddled on the floor, his naked body heaving. He looked as if he was sobbing, with powerful wracking spasms rippling through his body.

Steiner had walked out of the death camps where six million others hadn't, maybe he would never really escape, thought Keel and began to turn over.

Then he heard the cracks, like Chinese firecrackers going off at a dragon dance. Rapid fire, one after another. Steiner arched up into a kneeling position, hands falling from his sunken chest. His torso looked lumpy and misshapen. Keel realized with horror that Steiner had cracked his own ribs. Keel thought of screaming for the guard's, but knew it would be futile. The screws never ventured near the cells at night.

Steiner looked up at Keel, his gargoyle face like a rock in the moonlight. He was breathing hard. Bubbling.

'Aaaah, it hurts so..'

'It's the only way Keel. The only way of breaking out. Have to break out before the doctors come.'

Steiner shuffled to the wall below the window. The wind outside howled and spat dust into the cell. As the moonlight caught Steiner through a break in the clouds, Keel saw that his thighs and shins were busted, broken bones moved in his legs like clenched fists under rubber. The flesh had discoloured into black and purple blotches.

'I'm getting out Keel.'

Steiner swung himself in a low arc, slamming the whitewashed brick with the side of his head, leaving a bloody smear. His bald cranium crumpled like an egg. Steiner lay still, his flesh tensed and torn at odd points by the white bone.

Then Steiner jigged up, as if tugged up by wires, standing unsteadily like a marionette. His head slumped back so that the highest point of Steiner's body was the jut of his Adam's apple. The vertebrae below Steiner's skull must have been shattered.

Keel backed into the darkest corner of his bunk. He was caught in a nightmare. He wanted to scream but only a strangled cry escaped from his lips.


Steiner raised his claw like hand and Keel saw the flash of an old-fashioned razor blade. The hand slashed down and Steiner sighed in agony, as he methodically used the blade to sever the flesh around each joint. The silver scars that circled Steiner's body erupted red behind the steel.

'I'm getting out.', he burbled again, blowing bloody froth from his mouth. The blade scythed down Steiner's chest and abdomen splitting him open like an overripe fruit. Broken ribs jutted out and intestines uncoiled like an orgy of wet snakes.

Then Steiner proceeded to break the rest of his bones, swinging his torso so that he cracked sickeningly against the walls, sparing only the blade wielding hand. Steiner carved himself behind the ears and his fingers dug into his skull extracting shards of bone. His head collapsed like a deflating football. Half shuffling, half sliding he turned to Keel. His lips hanging like the downturned smile of a clown and now funneling like blow hole.

'A bone for a bone for a bone.' Then with agonizing patience, Steiner began to extract each broken bone from his body.

Eventually all that remained of Steiner was a bloody, collapsed mass of tissue that looked like a burst waterbed, still attached to his small bird like hand. The hand clawed inch by slow inch up to the barred window, dragging the rest of Steiner up with it. The burst and carved tissue distorted like a water filled balloon as it squeezed through the bars. Thick pink fluid sprayed the cell, splattering Keel and his gallery of page 3 cut outs on the wall. The stench of blood and shit thickened the air.

Keel finally screamed as Steiner's head squeezed through, popping eyes and exuding phlegm marbled red and purple, through the flat slits that had been Steiner's nose. Keel trembled violently as he watched the thing that was Steiner flap back and forth outside the cell anchored only be the clawed hand.

Finally, the wind took Steiner, whipping him into the sky like a wet blanket, twisting and turning. His flapping mass dipped and rose erratically over the prison wall, and then out of sight. Keel saw it again, in the far distance. Steiner seemed to have gained some sort of control, his arms and legs spread like a kite. Hovering in the grey light of dawn.

Keel knew that Steiner was waiting, hovering like some ghastly vampire, bur not for blood. He wanted new bones.

They found Keel in the morning, huddled in a foetal ball, by turns moaning and whispering, 'Sweet Jesus and Mary, mother of god - protect me,' over and over again and compulsively cracking his knuckles as if counting prayers on a rosary.

The End.

# Bogeyman

## Joshua Parrott

Physician: Dr. Peterson
8268-WCT29

This can't be happening. This can't be happening. This can't be happening. This can't be happening. This can't be happening. This can't be happening. This can't be happening. This can't be happening. This can't be happening. This can't be happening. This can't be happening. This can't be happening. This can't be happening. This can't be happening.

------

SIDS. That's what the medical examiner had called it. Our daughter, Meredith, had died at nearly six months old because of some random, unexplainable, mishap. With all their modern technology to flaunt in front of you the modern medical practitioner is still nothing but a witch doctor in a hut, rattling bones at you. Modern science is utter bullshit.

I feel like an asshole even saying it but Meredith's death hit my wife, Jackie, much harder than it did me. That's not to say I wasn't broke up, I was, extremely so, but Jackie was devastated. She was the one who found her that morning. I had been at work dealing with a huge backlog of reports from the few weeks I took off from my job at Bryceland Security to spend with my wife and newborn. The neighbors later told me they could hear her screams from inside their own homes, violent and frantic at first, and then more and more hollow as she bundled Meredith in the car and drove to the hospital. I received a call at work from some desk nurse and rushed to the hospital only to find my wife asleep. Apparently, she was so hysterical that the doctor had to issue her sedative. The doctor told me exactly what the medical examiner would confirm later. Jackie woke up after an hour or so and, thankfully, didn't resume her screaming. She buried herself into my shoulder and wept. She wept with full abandon and she hasn't really stopped. Our daughter died six months ago and still my wife's tears keep a steady vigil for our Meredith.

I understood, at first. I'm not a monster, for god's sake. But *you* have to understand that after months of wailing, your concern can start getting tinged with a bit of annoyance. I had taken two days off. That, plus my weekend, was about all I could do after taking all that time off when Meredith was born. Just enough time to bury my daughter and spend a few days trying to find the road towards normal again. But it was clear that Jackie could not be left alone. Her tears came in bouts which swung between quiet sobbing to hysterical wailing. It became a daily battle just to get her to drink enough water to remain hydrated, let alone get her to eat anything. She had been an only child and both her parents had been gone since before we met. There was nobody else. So, what could I do? What in the hell were my options? Sick day after sick day were used. What little vacation time I had left saved was quickly burned through. After a month I was let go with a terribly small severance package.

But I didn't mind! Please know that. I fear I'm coming across as the biggest dick in the universe, but my only worry at the time really was the well-being of my wife. "Jobs come and go," I told myself. "She'll be back to normal in no time," was another familiar phrase running through my head at the time. Yet days turned to weeks, and weeks to months. Jackie lost weight quickly and took full time to her bed. Doctors came and told me the obvious. She needs to calm down. She needs to eat. She needs to start moving around the house. Whether Jackie could hear their advice, whether she could understand the consequences of what she was doing, I'll never know. I don't think she even knew the doctors were there. Her eyes clamped down shut as her body heaved violently with each new outburst. I'd bet money she couldn't even hear the doctors through the sound of her own sobs. But then, just a bit ago, she stopped. It took me awhile to notice what had changed, I had become so accustomed to the sound. You'd think I'd be happy, that this was a good thing. But after what I just saw I'd gladly die a thousand times, in the most horrible ways imaginable, just to hear her crying echo down from upstairs.

Earlier tonight I was trying to get some sleep on the floor of Meredith's nursery. I'm sorry to say that it wasn't out of any need to feel closer to my departed daughter but from the need to get away from my ridiculous wife. I mean, six months. Six months! Who cries for six months? I was becoming a little crazy from it, I admit. My only hope at getting some rest was to get away from my wife so I angrily grabbed at my pillows, yanked the comforter off of her, and curled up on the nursery floor atop of the furry, bunny throw rug Jackie had found so cute. But even there, across the hall, I could hear every whine and sniffle. Putting the pillow over my head still offered no relief. Out of sheer frustration I threw four hard punches into the bunny's face. Finally, I gave up and went downstairs to make myself a drink. If she wouldn't let me sleep, I'd just drink until I passed out.

The ever-present sobs were still audible down in the living room, but they were muffled and easier to deal with. After my third scotch they became just another background noise, like the hum of the refrigerator. I took stock of our living room. In the recent months I had been forced to sell off a lot of our possessions. A hysterical wife and no job will do that. The living room was quickly becoming as bare as when we moved in. Gone were the Blu-ray player, the collection of movies, and the 64" television. Next sold, in a passive aggressive move on my part I admit, was the antique curio that belonged to my wife's mother and her collection of music boxes that went all the way back to her great-great grandmother. I felt no small amount of guilt when I found out how much they were worth, but it was quickly assuaged when the cash was in my hand. I had even sold off most the furniture set, keeping only the small loveseat in hopes that Jackie might come downstairs and lay in it instead. Other than that, the only other objects in the room was the computer sitting on the card table in the corner with a folding lawn chair in front of it. I knew I would have to sell it soon. It and the car were my only big-ticket items left and I couldn't sell the car. What if I had to dive Jackie to the hospital? It was an ever-growing possibility. So, the computer would have to be next.

I drained my scotch. The sobbing upstairs dulled a little more as I poured another and sat down in front of the computer, quickly moving the mouse to get rid of the screensaver. It was a picture of Meredith, Jackie, and myself, taken the day we brought Meredith home from the hospital. In the picture Jackie's eyes were bright and dry, her mouth stretched into one of her huge, teeth bearing grins. She's cradling Meredith in her arms, a "Welcome Home" banner hanging behind her. Just to the right of her is me. Standing there with a look of quiet terror. I'd stared at this picture enough in the past months. Quickly I set to the task of saving things I wanted to keep onto disc. Folder after folder was saved and then deleted, when my eyes fell upon an icon I'd forgotten about. Shortly after we'd brought Meredith home, I'd gone into the office to retrieve a program. It was a program we called Home Protect, and all it is is a simple surveillance program. It allowed me to put a small webcam in the nursery so that we'd be able to monitor Meredith from the downstairs computer, from my work computer, or even our phones. A high-tech nanny cam, if you will. It would record 24 hours a day and keep the data, off site, stored for six months, ready to view for anyone with the password. Before I could think about what I was doing I typed it in.

There on the screen was the frozen image of my daughter. She was lying on her back in her crib, little fists in the air, one leg kicked out, motionless and just begging me to press play and bring her to life. I have no idea why but I actually glanced at the ceiling, to the room where my wife laid crying. Was I looking for permission? Was I hoping she would stop her tears and join me? I turned back to the screen and braced myself. I hit play. Instantly Meredith came to life. Punching and kicking in the air while her insistent cries poured quietly out of my desktop speakers. My eyes started to well up instantly. I downed my scotch in an attempt to hold back the waterworks but just as I did the darkened room on the screen lit up as my Jackie walked through the door and up to the crib. The tears flowed freely down my cheeks as I heard her soft voice saying words of comfort, words of love, to my baby girl. She picked her up and, holding her close, rocked her back and forth while humming gently against Meredith's head. With every breath Jackie took I could see her inhale our daughter's scent, a oh-so-content smile on her lips. Jackie looked so full of life, so like the Jackie I loved. Just at that moment a particularly loud wail issued from upstairs and before I could stop myself, I screamed, "SHUT UP!" at the ceiling as loud as I could. But the real Jackie only cried louder. By the time I turned back to the monitor both Jackie and Meredith were gone.

I spent hours fast forwarding and rewinding the video feed, bringing both Jackie and Meredith back to life, while the real Jackie remained unreachable to me, crying into her pillow. A few more scotches, (I was feeling a bit drunk by that point,) and I was ready to face the truth. That I was just preparing myself to look at my daughter's final night. To watch the life leave her body. If I had known what I was about to witness I can't honestly say I would have watched it.

I punched in the date and settled on the time of 9pm. There lay Meredith. Fast asleep and obviously breathing. I lingered there for a moment and then fast forwarded to 10pm. Still she lay asleep with her chest rising and falling gently. I kept pushing on through the hours, holding my breath each time I was about to hit play.

Then, somewhere between one and two, something appeared in the bedroom with her. I quickly hit rewind and then play. There was my daughter, just beginning to cry, not even loud enough to reach Jackie's mommy-ears, when the closet door opened slowly. Meredith heard it and quieted a little, probably expecting her mother or me, but when neither one of us appeared she began to whimper softly again. Then, (I couldn't believe what I was seeing and wondered if the scotch was to blame,) a dog walked out of the closet. It was a mix of colors, all very dull. Greys, blacks, and browns seemingly swirling together. Its head was far too small for its body. Just as my head was asking what the hell a dog was doing in my daughter's room, my stomach turned with the knowledge that this was not a dog. It had eight legs, each leg having four joints, and when it walked it would stick one leg out at a time, fully extend all four joints and then drop it to the floor. First its front left leg, then the front right, and further on down it's torso, which seemed to extend and contract with its movements. Bile and scotch burned the back of my throat but I could not tear my eyes away from the screen. I zoomed in on the creature and sat, breathless and more frightened then I'd ever been, afraid to even breathe as I saw the creature's head up close. What, from a distance, had appeared as a stunted, small appendage at the end of its torso was something much worse. The head was in fact made up of dozens of small tentacles, like an octopus's, swirling over each other in dizzying frenzy. Every so often one would reach out in front of the creature as if feeling its way. It climbed vertically up the crib and slowly crawled towards Meredith. My eyes had ceased their tears with a kind of sick wonderment but the bile sat firmly in the back of my mouth. I watched, eyes wide, and frozen in my seat, a cold sweat on my upper lip as it climbed on top of Meredith. For a moment Meredith calmed down, unsure of what was happening. She then began to cry ever so softly but building and building. But before it would have been loud enough to wake us, the... thing, extended a long, black tongue from within its maze of tentacles and proceeded to cover Meredith's face as it lapped at her tears. The vomit came immediately and fell over my keyboard and shirt. Still, I could not look away. Meredith's cries were reduced to soundless tears as the creature fed. Suddenly the monsters tongue shot back behind the tentacles and Meredith lay still. The tears had not returned when, as I watched, two of the tentacles near the back of its horrid head reached forward towards Meredith. They hovered over her face momentarily and then plunged into my baby's tiny ears. The sick knowledge that the creature was only trying to make my baby produce more tears for its feast was quickly proven true, for no sooner had Meredith let out a cry then the tentacles withdrew from her ears and the horrid black tongue re-emerged to lap at her face. Its body seemed to shutter with ecstasy as Meredith's grew stiller and stiller. Again, her cries grew softer and body lay still. The creature removed it's tongue again and started to back off of her. Suddenly it stopped and plunged the two tentacles into her tiny ears again, much further in than I would have thought possible. Meredith didn't cry out. Meredith didn't move. Satisfied, the creature removed its tentacles and with its slow, jerky walk, made its exit back into the closet. Meredith lay in her crib. Her tiny chest completely still.

I sat in a state of pure shock. My mind racing, trying to put the pieces of what I'd just seen into some form that resembled the world I knew. I pressed stop on the computer and the house went quiet, the only sound was the dull thud of my vomit dripping onto the carpet. It dawned on me. Much slower than I wished it had, but slowly my head swiveled towards the stairs. Dazed, I crept towards the staircase, straining my ears to pick up any sound in the house. Once I reached the foot of the stairs, I craned my neck forward, tilting my head, struggling to hear upstairs.

Silence.

And then...

A tiny muted cry coming from our bedroom, that's quickly smothered by something wet.

------

Now I'm running up the stairs as fast as I can. There is no sound of crying. There is no sound in the house at all. The only thing I can hear is the voice in my head repeating over and over, *"This can't be happening. This can't be happening. This can't be happening."*

The End.

# The Lake

## William Hage

Physician: Dr. Peterson
8268-WCT20

Charlie sat on one of the benches, barraged by the ridiculing laughter of the surrounding geese. He knew it was just a sound they made; one he had heard numerous times in the past. In this moment, however, it was laughter; it was laughter solely for him. It was not for the families with children that played around the lake enjoying the one nice day of the week. Dozens, hundreds of cackles in response to a joke he didn't know the beginning to. He knew only the punch line. It was him.

Charlie noticed an odd but familiar odor fill the air around him. It took less than thirty seconds for his brain to inform him the smell was bleach. *Why would I smell bleach out here?* There were plenty of people around, but no houses or businesses that could produce the smell. With that, the thought and odor were gone and it was back to the laughing.

Trying to ignore it he scanned the lake, watching the children play in the water. The families seemed happy picnicking, using the provided grills to cook food. Charlie had visited the same lake with his own family, but those times were far gone.

On the other side of the lake he noticed something in the tall grass. Maybe the grass was something else. It was at least five feet high, but to Charlie it was just really tall grass. First, he only noticed the color blue, then he saw the blue belonged to the shorts of a small boy playing in the grass. The child could have been no more than five or six. Charlie thought of how the grass towered over him. He could not figure out why but the child in the grass brought apprehension to him, as if this plant had some insidious intentions. There was a sense of ominous foreboding like the grass was going to swallow the child whole. Or maybe like a million razors, they will cut into the boy's flesh, spraying blood into the air. He looked around and saw no adults near the boy, not even other children. Even if he called out across the lake, the others would probably just think he was crazy. He was the only one with the vantage point to see the child.

*Where are his damn parents? Who just leaves a five-year-old at a lake to their own devices?*

The boy was still making his way through the grass towards the lake. All Charlie could see was the grass ready to devour this small child. Charlie was on the bank of the lake now, not even recalling that he had left his bench and walked fifteen feet to the edge of the lake. The boy was only a foot or two away from the bank on his own side.

*Yes get in the water, get away from that damn grass!*

First the child's right leg broke the surface sending a small wave of ripples out into the water. His left foot followed.

*Hurry, hurry, you're still too close to that grass!* Charlie could feel the scream in his throat even though the words were only spoken in his mind.

The wind blew in, sending the grass downward towards the boy. "No!" He could no longer see the boy. He could only see the malevolent grass. The geese rose up in another chorus of laughter. "Shut up," Charlie said. The wind subsided and the grass returned to its natural position.

Charlie fell to his knees sinking slightly into the sandy bank of the lake. He clutched at his chest as a sigh of relief crossed his face. He let out a small exhale of breath. The boy was in the lake now up to his waist unharmed by the sinister grass. Charlie took a deep breath and shuddered on the exhale.

As he stood Charlie saw something breach the surface of the water. It looked like an arm, but the color was of it was yellow and green. *What the hell?* He watched as the appendage wrapped around the boy's waist and pulled him under. "No! Someone help him." He was sure that he spoke the words aloud, but no one reacted. Most of the people were off to his right side from where he stood. He could reach the boy quicker by going to the left.

Charlie ran as fast as his overweight aging body would permit. What took maybe two minutes felt like ten to him. The boy's arms still thrashed around; whatever it was seemed to allow the boy to briefly come to the surface. Charlie waded into the water and his nostrils were assaulted by the smell of bleach again. He grabbed onto the boy's arm as it was being dragged down again. The power of whatever held the boy was immense no match for Charlie's own feeble frame, but he would not relent. Suddenly the pulling stopped whether his own adrenaline kicked in or whatever had its hold let go he was not sure. The sudden change sent Charlie flying backwards into the water. Something came up, just a hint of black, until the boy's face rose above the surface. He was sobbing and screaming. Charlie grabbed the boy and helped him to the edge of the bank. In the distance he saw that some of the people were now looking over at them.

Charlie let out a sigh. It was over. Help was on the way and he would be the hero that saved the boy. With all of the commotion, he did not realize that his legs were still in the water. Something large swam between his legs and brushed up against them. "Oh shit." The yellow arm came out of the water, barely creating a splash as it wrapped around Charlie's leg and pulled him under. He tried to scream for help but his mouth only filled with water. He fought as hard as he could briefly making it back to the surface letting out a faint cry for help before he was pulled under again. Through the glassy water he could see a crowd of people around the body as he continued to sob with his hands over his eyes. *Tell them. Tell them*

*I saved you. Tell them I need help!* Everyone was focused on the boy. They didn't even appear to know that Charlie was struggling just beneath the surface.

Another arm swam directly in front of Charlie's face. It was quick, but he could see that it was not really an arm. The closest his brain could define it would be a tentacle. It was long and tapered off into a point. *What…what the fuck is that?* The tentacle came around again this time entering Charlie's mouth and going down his throat. He choked, gagging as his arm frantically tried to pry the thing from his mouth. Charlie's fingernails punctured the exterior of the tentacle a green inky liquid seeped out, but it held its place. He tried to scream, feeling the vibrations in his throat against the appendage that was now wiggling its way down into his stomach. Charlie's last thought before everything went black was why he was not gasping for air any longer.

Then the darkness took over.

Charlie woke on the bank of the lake there was a crowd of people standing around him gawking.

"What is it?" he heard a woman say.

"Hell if I know," a man said. "Looks a little bit like a fish… only a hell of a lot bigger."

Charlie sat up and everyone in the crowd stepped back. There were a few gasps amidst the only other sound: the laughter of the geese. He coughed and water spewed out of his mouth. He raised a hand to his face, but it wasn't his hand any longer. It was yellow and green, webbing connecting the discolored fingers that were now at least two inches longer. *What the hell is going on?*

"What the fuck are you?" a man said, standing a few feet away with a large rock in his hand.

Charlie spoke, but the words were unintelligible sounding like someone trying to talk with a gulp of water in the back of their mouth.

The man raised the rock but a woman standing next to him grabbed his arm. "What are you doing?" she said.

"We don't know what this thing is! We should kill it before it tries to kill us." the man said.

"Maybe it's harmless. It looks scared."

"Harmless? Look at the fucking thing, it looks like some kinda damn fish. Look at those big black eyes, there's no soul behind eyes like that." A few of the other men murmured in agreement following suit and also picking up rocks.

The first rock sent Charlie's head to the side. It didn't hurt like he expected it to; it merely stung a bit. He put a webbed hand to what would be his forehead and when he brought the hand back down it was covered in an inky green ooze. *What is happening to me? What?*

*Why? What did I ever do? I tried to help that damn boy, he shouldn't have even been out here all alone.* Another rock came hitting him in the chest, then another, and another. The faces of the crowd had turned from confusion to anger.

Charlie knew he had to get out of there or the crowd would kill him, but there was no place to run except that lake. He rolled the few feet until his body was in the lake. As soon as he was in just a few feet of water his body felt lighter. His mobility seemed to increase and he was able to swim out twenty feet before another stone was thrown. The crowd was still throwing them when he submerged. *How long will they wait? How long can I stay under here?* It was a full minute before Charlie realized that he was not holding his breath. Instead, he was breathing perfectly fine. He didn't question it, it didn't really matter anymore. There were too many questions without answers.

The bottom of the lake was only blackness. Charlie never really thought the lake was that deep although he had never actually tested it. He began to effortlessly swim down to the bottom; his body being swallowed by the darkness. He didn't stop until the surface was no longer visible. The tentacle came right by his face, but it didn't attack this time. To Charlie it appeared as if it was pointing. He followed its directions and swam deeper into the darkness.

The End.

# The House Lights Dim

**Tim Major**

Physician: Dr. Peterson
S268-WCT29

Before the bright light were the migraines. Nobody quite agreed when they had begun. The first accounts had been buried deep in the later pages of the daily newspapers. Those afflicted told of piercing squalls of pain and the sensation of internal, growing pressure.

As luck would have it, the first high-profile case was a newsreader. He had been struck with dizziness and pain during an evening broadcast. The image of a familiar face wracked with anguish became the one most associated with the outbreak. In the days following the broadcast the footage spread across the internet, sweeping first Britain and then the world. Thousands more cases of spontaneous migraines were reported.

There were many different opinions about the causes. The most vague, and yet widely-held, was that a critical mass of everyday worries and strains had been reached. Modern society had introduced so many extra stresses on the average person that, in an instant, the mind could rebel and simply shut down. More imaginative versions of this argument added that while the first cases were spontaneous, the later ones had been triggered by the first in a wave of sympathetic, but unconscious, identification.

Other views were more extreme. Several religious groups claimed that the migraines were evidence of visitations by their respective deities. Some suggested that humans were being punished for specific sins ranging from interference in foreign affairs, to the debasement of marriage, to the worshipping of rival gods.

I followed the story only half-heartedly. In fact, in those days everything I did was conducted with little enthusiasm. My wife, Catherine, had finally left me, after many months of troubles bubbling under, only weeks before the migraine story broke. Afterwards, I asked myself whether my views on children were really so strongly held. The image of Catherine and I as parents quickly lost any of its sense of compromise or defeat and became, rather, an unattainable ideal. Rationally, the thought of having borne children and then being in the same situation filled me with horror. There's no way that I could have disciplined children to the degree that I began to discipline myself.

***

I had been working in my study – the room that Catherine would have designated the nursery – on the morning of the burst of light. I'd arranged to conduct my proofreading work from home, giving the excuse that my wife was ill and needed regular attention, but in Catherine's absence the real reason was more linked to the attention I gave to my wine collection. These were desperately unhappy days and I remember little about the texts that passed beneath my bleary eyes.

At that moment, I had not even been looking at my manuscript. Instead, I gazed blankly out of the window behind my desk. The cul-de-sac was quiet as usual. The only sign of life was an elderly neighbour struggling to restore his large wheelie bin to its correct position. I didn't consider the possibility of helping him.

When it happened, the thought flashed through my mind that I was blacking out. I'd drunk myself into a stupor several times in the preceding weeks, but this was mid-morning and I was sober. The piercing brightness washed over me and I was submerged in a sea of light. My eyes flickered shut but the effect was minimal, as if I had closed my eyelids while gazing upwards on an intensely bright summer's day. I held up a hand to shield myself from the light pouring from the wide window. My fingers appeared as thin grey silhouettes, haloed with absolute whiteness.

***

I don't know how long I lay unconscious on the carpeted floor of the study. It couldn't have been for more than a day, as there was no sense of hunger when I awoke. Even with my eyes still closed I perceived the overwhelmingly bright light that continued to stream in from the window. A pain in my forehead throbbed in regular pulses, seconds apart.

Tentatively, I opened one eye a fraction. The pain doubled and my right hand raised instinctively to cup my eyes. Under my palm I felt the dampness of my swollen cheeks and tears ran in rivulets through my fingers. Despite the monotonous ache in my temples, I felt certain that these were not the symptoms of the widely-reported migraines: the light pouring in from the window was tangible and searing.

I discovered later that the curtains had been tightly closed. When Catherine and I had prepared to go on our final holiday abroad together I had been in the grip of a fear for the security of our house. After installing a cheap – and, as it turns out, faulty – alarm system and timed, automated curtain closers at the two front-facing windows, I had lost interest. The curtains were heavy and thick but the light penetrated them as if they were tissue paper. Without their presence I'm not certain that I would have regained consciousness at all.

I kept one hand clamped over my face as my other groped around the small sofa beside my desk. That morning I had returned from a short walk (excruciating, due to my hangover) and then had come directly to my study. I pushed away the coat that hung limply from the seat and from underneath grasped the woollen scarf abandoned there. I fought against another spell of faintness as I crawled weakly under the table with my face turned away from the window. I grimaced and closed my eyes tightly, then used both hands to wrap the scarf four or five times around my head.

My eyes protested at the tension upon them but the scarf did much to relieve the waves of discomfort. Light still burned my retinas but felt manageable. Blindly, I swept my arm to clear the desk. On the right-hand side of the room was a low bookcase. As quickly as I could manage, I ripped the books from it and hefted the case onto the desk, stumbling on loose volumes underfoot. The bookcase fitted the window frame almost perfectly. Once it was in place, I loosened my mask to survey my work. The room was now bathed in an eerie grey light, with none of the warmth of a summer's day. I could perceive the outline of the bookcase, although I kept my gaze away from the knife-edge of light still creeping in at the sides. I pulled the scarf back into position, curled up on the sofa with the coat over my head to block out more of the light, and I slept.

My first instinct when I awoke was to turn on the portable radio. Twisting the dial afforded no interruption to the jeering static. As the light had not abated, I moved from room to room cautiously, blind due to the scarf still covering my eyes. I struggled to barricade each room against the seeping light using wardrobes, upturned tables and other such objects. My head continued to throb and each successive room introduced new levels of discomfort.

When, after much gritting of teeth, I had reached the end of the corridor leading to the glass-panelled front door I forced myself to pause before applying the thick layers of cardboard that I had reclaimed from the garage. I opened the door a crack and moved my head to the opening, my eyes averted. The cul-de-sac was always quiet, but the silence outside was eerie and complete. I realised that in ordinary circumstances I would have been able to hear the distant hum of the main road that passed through the residential estate. Now, nothing. Even the sound of birds in the trees was absent. I called out into the void, with no response except the tinny echo of my own voice.

When the house was secured, I retreated to the kitchen, feeling my way as I still didn't dare to remove the scarf from my eyes. I thought to turn on the small television set on the counter. The box hummed into life for only a moment, then sputtered and died. The electric oven failed to power up for even a second. I found and opened a tin of peaches and ate greedily. Then I sat on the bench at the kitchen table, rested my head on the crook of my arm, and slept once more.

***

I sit in the same room now. It's changed beyond all recognition. There are wooden planks nailed to the wall to my right, totally obscuring the single small window. I'm resting in a wing-back armchair taken from the lounge. The lounge is the largest room in the house, but has proved uninhabitable. Not only does it have a large window at the north end, at the south is a patio door leading to a conservatory. The white light outside carries no heat, but the conservatory seems to magnify its intensity to a degree that no amount of barricades can block totally.

If I remain within the other rooms in the house I am able to use my eyes again, more or less. Rather than the woollen scarf of those early days, I now wear a gauze bandage over my eyes. This lessens the intensity of the light but still allows me to make out the shapes of objects within the house. I have become used to a monochrome view of this limited world. My hands have become as adept at seeing as my eyes.

I soon identified the kitchen as the room best insulated against the light, so it is where I rest after my chores are complete. On a low table beside my chair is a gramophone inherited from my parents. The only records that I own also once belonged to them. Listening to music at a particular time each day has become a tradition, a way of marking the passing of time in the absence of evening's darkness.

Very little space in the kitchen is used for food preparation nowadays as most of my meals are eaten raw. I soon realised that my stores of tinned food would not last long. I remember the struggle of transplanting some of the crops in my garden allotment to the row of pots now squatting just outside the back door. Even with my face protected with a scarf and thick blanket, I barely made it back to the safety of the house after each trip. Moving the crops was a shrewd move, as the light outside seems only to have intensified month to month. The plants grow at extraordinary speeds although rain is scarce so they need regular watering. Some days I feel unable to face the influx of light as I open the door to tend to them. I eat less and less, and when I look in the mirror my silhouette appears hopelessly gaunt.

I find myself wondering how widespread the plague of light may be. Does the disabling of power and communications systems indicate that the whole world is affected, or just Britain? I know little about physics but if the Sun had become more powerful, shouldn't it have enveloped the Earth totally? Sometimes this line of thought leads me to a conviction that I, along with everyone and everything else, really did perish in a sunburst, and that I am simply a ghostly echo of my former life. Similarly, I sometimes spend days convinced that the light is simply a trick of the mind and that I have inflicted this madness upon myself. Or perhaps, after all, I am simply suffering from the same migraines that afflicted so many others. Otherwise, what connects the migraines and the plague of light?

How many other people survive still? It has been eight months now. Many of those who managed to feed themselves initially must have been seen off by the winter chill. Might Catherine still be alive? I often lie awake in bed looking up at the streaks of escaped light upon my ceiling and imagine that I can feel her pressing against me, fidgeting in her sleep.

My supplies won't last indefinitely. My stores of tinned food are almost totally depleted. The crops are yielding less each week due to my increasing reluctance to spare water for them. Incredibly, the taps in the kitchen still operate, but the quality of the water they provide is looking more and more suspect. Nowadays I use an arrangement of filters made from old towels to purify the liquid as much as possible.

Recently I have come to accept that I must venture beyond my own property to find more food. If I wait much longer, my strength will be diminished and my chance of success far lower. I have spent many days in the kitchen with maps of the neighbourhood spread over the table, examining them as closely as I am able to through my gauze mask.

A corner shop is situated only streets away from my house. In the past I found it of little use as its supplies of fresh fruit and vegetables were terribly limited. However, beyond the newspaper racks I recall shelves of tinned food. Catherine and I used to joke that some of them looked old enough to have been rations from the war. Now the thought of those same dusty tins of carrots and pineapple make my stomach leap in anticipation.

The standard route to the shop would have been to the left along the cul-de-sac, then right and right again onto the main road at the junction, tracing three sides of a square. I feel certain that I would not be able to take this route now without succumbing to the awful pressure of the piercing light. With the aid of the maps I identify a direct route to the shop. Only one house stands in my way if I were to turn to the right instead, walk to the end of the cul-de-sac and then navigate through that property and out the other side. It's still a great risk, but I'm also conscious that my neighbour's house itself may be a source of food and, at least, temporary shelter.

I gather together another roll of gauze, blankets, hats, winter coats and a large hiking rucksack. If I fail my chances of returning to the house will be low, so I gorge myself on the remaining vegetables, a cherished tin of butter beans, and a pint of distilled water. I wrap gauze around and around my head, then a scarf twisted thickly, then a woollen hat to hold it all in place. I carry the coat on my shoulders, ready to hoist it over my head. Even prepared like this, I gasp as I remove the cardboard from the front door and wrench it open.

Immediately, I feel the light seep through my eyelids and, I fancy, into my mind. The ringing in my ears that has been a dull constant now amplifies, further disorienting me. I shake my head balefully and begin to plod carefully towards the end of the road. The silence unnerves me. The only sounds I can hear are my uneven footsteps and ragged breathing. I clear my throat, hear the sound echo, and use it to estimate my distance from the houses on either side of the street. After a few metres I stumble. I pause only for a moment to reach down and touch something cold, yielding and rotten. I am strict with myself and do not allow myself to imagine what it may be.

I take several more steps before I detect the grass under my feet. The pain in my head is almost unbearable. Even with my eyes squeezed tight shut I feel as though I were staring directly at the bulb of a powerful lamp. But I am nearly at the fence and therefore halfway to my neighbour's house.

The fence is not high but I struggle to climb it due to dizziness and the unfamiliar exertion on my limbs. My trouser leg snags on the rough timber and for a moment I am inclined to rest there, uncomfortably straddling the fence, exhausted and accepting my fate. I throw my winter coat over the fence ahead of me in order to free both hands, which allows more light to assault me. With a great effort I hoist myself over, ripping my left trouser leg. I scrabble around for my coat and huddle for a minute in a shivering igloo of fabric.

In my previous life I avoided approaching this fence due to a small but vociferous pit bull terrier that patrolled its length. As I stand and set off again, I reason that the dog must surely have died long ago. I tell myself that no owner would prioritise a pet over their own welfare, and without vision the animal would have struggled to forage for food. More from weakness than caution, I cross the length of the garden on my hands and knees.

I pause every few paces to rest and clear my thoughts, fighting an overwhelming desire to lie down and sleep on the bare ground.

When I reach a concrete patio my heart leaps with all the joy it can muster. I drag myself forward and am suddenly terrified of encountering a locked door, or, worse still, one reinforced like the doors of my own house. But as my fingers reach to claw at the ledge, I find no obstacle. The door is wide open. With a giant effort I haul myself into the house and kick weakly to shut the door behind me. The light is not much diminished – there are no planks or barriers to block the light at the door's edges – but it is enough to allow me to lie panting and feel my energy restoring.

I sleep fitfully for some time, perhaps only minutes. I pull myself upright and move cautiously along the corridor. The house is built to the same specifications of all the others in the estate, but by stepping one pace into each room at the end of corridor I find that the linoleum floor, and therefore the kitchen, is on the opposite side to the one in my own house. The curtains in each room must be drawn, as the intensity of the light is less than outside, but I am still forced to leave my scarves and coat in place as I grope around. I encounter only crockery in the first two cupboards, but in the third I grasp at cold tins and dense cardboard containers. I place a couple onto the kitchen table and then fish around in my rucksack for the can opener and spoon within. As I open the first tin I give brief thanks to my absent host.

The spoon has not reached my lips when I hear a noise and freeze. It seems to come from within the building. At first I imagine that it is my neighbour, but then I remember the full cupboards and my breathing becomes shallow and fast. Then – again – there! It comes from within the main part of the house and sounds like air escaping sharply from something under pressure. Some semblance of calm returns to me. Perhaps some long-abandoned gadgetry is still operational somewhere within the building? But still I do not begin eating.

The third time, the noise is definitely closer to hand. The hissing sound is low and ends with a languorous rattle. A chill descends upon me. My head turns from side to side as I listen, trying to locate the source of the sound, which rings out twice more.

Even before it occurs again, I sense that the source of the noise is now within the kitchen. I hold my breath and fight the urge to pull the scarves from my face to try to catch a glimpse of whatever is now in the room with me. Perhaps it has the same instinct, as there is a tense quiet and the only sound I can hear is a gentle tapping of something settling on the linoleum. Then, the eerie hiss and rattle, which now seems intense and malevolent. Should I strike out? I'm conscious that I'm trapped in a seated position behind the large table and, comically, I am brandishing only a spoon.

When it comes, the movement is a swift flurry. After a frenzy of tapping on the linoleum the creature strikes. I bolt from my chair, tipping over the table and then I swing the coat from my head. I feel the heavy fabric swat at something angular and hard before it gets tangled – or snatched – and I move quickly to dodge around the perimeter of the room, aiming for the doorway. Just as I reach it my left foot is pulled backwards sharply. My head strikes the ground but the impact is softened by the thick scarves still wound tightly around my eyes.

My left foot is caught on something and my thrashing does nothing to dislodge it. In my panic I realise that the flesh at my ankle is being pinched roughly from either side. I hear a tapping noise on the linoleum beside me and then, with a start, I sense something scratching for purchase amid the bundle of fabric around my head. I struggle and kick fruitlessly. Before the scarves are torn away the creature makes a rasping cackle that I liken to a cry of triumph or the death rattle of a cobra.

Immediately, light pours into my eyes. I am left flailing in a white void and my limbs seem remote and out of my control. The throbbing within my head almost obscures the sickly clacking of the creature. Somehow, I wrest myself away and then I am stumbling along the corridor, bouncing from one wall to the other and limping badly. Some still-alert part of my brain reminds me that this house is a mirror image of my own and I turn into the corridor, bursting through the front door without recalling opening it. The rattle behind me has become feverish.

There is no sense of triumph in my escape. Without the scarves binding my eyes I am immediately disoriented once I am in the street. Not only do I not know where to run, I struggle to keep conscious of the fact that I <u>must</u> run and that I am in danger.

A calm settles upon me. Either I have left the rattling noise behind or it has stopped. The street is deathly quiet. I realise dimly that I must be standing across the street from my destination, the corner shop, but then I become woolly and distracted by the peculiar absence of birdsong. The light becomes a squall of white noise in my head, pulsing in time with my ragged breathing. I fall to the ground and roll onto my back, struggling to fill my lungs.

I surprise myself a little when the word 'Catherine' escapes my dry lips. I speak dully but the word echoes unnaturally, returning with a ringing, metallic tone. My eyes flicker open weakly. I am facing directly upwards. As I feel my energy disappear, I imagine that I perceive distinctions in the burning, pulsating light, as if there is not one, but many separate sources of the fierce whiteness. As unconsciousness edges down upon me, the waves of noise seem to become the scrapes of unseen mechanisms.

It's not so unbearable after all. The light warms me. I smile.


The End.

# Dark Verse

Physician: Dr. Salam
7128-DV758JJ

## Irene Mathias
## Rob Salem

The House on the hill is black and tall, with a hundred windows, round and small. It watches the village and forest below – A forest where only the bravest will go.

Down in the village live John, Jill and James. They're always playing "I dare you to" games. "Our dare today," the boys said to Jill, "go into the House on the top of the hill."

To their Useful Things bags they add water and food, then they walk arm-in-arm to the hill through the wood. "KEEP OUT!" warns a sign which was painted in red and surrounded by weeds and long grass that was dead.

But James just ignored it and pushed the gate wide, and its creaking hinge muffled a moan from inside! At the door he turned round, gave his last ever grin.

He said "Back in a minute" then he waltzed right on in.

John and Jill waited, then waited some more....
...and waited for James to walk back through the door. "He's trying to scare us." said John with a smile. "He'll soon get fed up, let's just wait for a while."

So they waited and waited and waited some more, but no James appeared at the big black oak door. "I'll get him." said John as he pushed the door wide. He waved his last wave as he vanished inside.

Jill restlessly waited, then waited some more
for both of her brothers to pounce through the door.
Then all of a sudden it started to pour.

The heavens erupted, the wind wildly roared. As she sat on
the porch to keep out of the rain,
Jill thought she heard John and James calling her name.
"Jill! Come and find us – that is if you dare!"
She opened the door and yelled "Brothers Beware!"

Her very last thought as she stepped through the door
-       "From tomorrow I won't play these games any more!"
The House on the hill is haunted still,
by John and James and their young sister Jill.

An eternity, it seems,
– or only a moment? –
have I borne this burden,
this work of sorrow
ceaseless in its being.
Upon a field
grey and lifeless
I am bound,
and there I harvest
the newborn soul.
Memory is not mine,
only the knowing
of what has been
and what must be,
and that, for me,
an eternity of being
is an end to the beginning.

On the
Record

# A Moment With Mainak Dhar

*We would like to introduce a writer who not only switches*

*between fiction and non-fiction but also between genres effortlessly. The book that kick-started his journey was a stapled together collection of Maths Solutions and Poems, which he created whilst in 7th Grade.*

*Since then he has moved on to thrillers, business books and finally Horror. In March 2013, became the #1 bestselling Horror author on Amazon, momentarily unseating Stephen King. We are really pleased to be spending a moment with Mainak Dhar.*

*What was your first experience of the horror genre?*

The first horror book I remember reading was Nightmares & Dreamscapes, the collection of short stories by Stephen King. The one story that stuck in my mind was The Night Flyer.

When you were growing up in was there a particular genre of horror that you would always seek out?

Not really. I read a lot of Stephen King, but other than that, my staple fare was not so much horror as an eclectic mix of fantasy (Tolkein), Roald Dahl and science and sci-fi (Asimov, Sagan).

*We mentioned that you started writing very young, are there any works that you go back and look at and want to release them?*

There was a short story I wrote when I was twelve called The Martyr, which was inspired by the news reports I read about how child soldiers, kids no older than me at the time, were being sent on suicide missions in the Iran Iraq war. Made me wonder about how messed up we were as a civilization if we didn't think twice about sacrificing our kids. That story lay in my computer for years, and I always wanted to see it in print, because unfortunately, in all those years, we haven't really improved much in terms of throwing away young lives in meaningless wars. What was cool that last year I got an opportunity to publish it in an anthology and I updated it to place it in the modern Afghan context, and I had the pleasure of seeing the earliest fiction I can remember writing (or at any rate, retaining), in print after so many years.

*Do you have a set schedule or routine when you sit down to write?*

With a full time day job and a family I want to spend quality time with, I do need to discipline myself to some extent. My broad routine is to ideate when I run in the morning and write for about thirty or forty-five minutes each night. I do travel a fair bit on my job, and I also get a lot of writing done in flights, airports and hotels.

*You recently released a new collection of short stories based in the "Deadland" world. How did you find changing from novels to short stories?*

It was pretty seamless for me, since I was writing in a world and about characters I had grown familiar with. My first foray was 'Off With Their Heads', a prequel where I wrote a short each about the background of each key character readers meet in Alice in Deadland, and how their lives were intertwined. That was a fun experience and so for Book 5 (Deadland: Untold Stories of Alice in Deadland), I returned to shorts, with a series of stories showing snapshots of Alice's life as she was growing up in the Deadland.

*There is talk that the "short's" time is drawing to a close, how do you feel about that statement?*

As a reader I will always be ready to read an engaging story independent of how long it is. If anything, the advent of ebooks makes for much more flexibility on formats and lengths. As a writer, I feel that shorts provide a great way of bringing in some 'relief' into a series by digging deeper into characters, side stories etc, which can enrich the total experience for the reader.

*Your work in the horror genre especially centres on a post-apocalyptic world. Is this a theme that you seem to stick to or are you planning to branch out?*

I'm really enjoying writing in the post apocalyptic genre, and will probably give it a go for a couple of more books. After that, let's see what strikes my fancy- I do have an idea for a dystopian series without zombies for a change, and get to it once I'm done with the latest book in the Alice series I'm working on.

*Zombies are big right now within popular culture, in your opinion what is going to be the next big thing?*

I think with the ever-growing concerns about how we're messing up our world, tinkering with nature, and also impinging on individual freedom in the name of security, dystopian fiction will probably be even more in focus. What specific form that takes or if a particular manifestation of it really takes off (like zombies did) is very hard to predict.

*You have several books out now – 13 I think at last count. Some are through publishers and some are self-published. What made you make the choice of self-publishing your "Alice in Deadland" books?*

Till 2011, I had several books published in India with major houses like Random House and Penguin, but when I brought my first Kindle and got to know about Amazon's self-publishing program, it opened my eyes to how I could reach international readers, and that's what led me to take the plunge into self-publishing.



For my first novel, I went through the school of hard knocks, accumulating close to fifty rejection slips, so I know just how tough it feels. I guess what helps is to have other things to keep you anchored and sane (in my case, my wife) and to keep writing. At that time, while my book was in limbo, I took up a part-time job writing a weekly column- kept my mind busy and my writing sharp. When that novel was picked up by a small press, and ultimately became a Bestseller in India, all that pain seemed worth it!



Most of my recent work has been in the horror genre, but for A Little Mayhem, I took a detour into a real horror far worse than zombies that so many Indian women face every day- the appalling state of affairs when it comes to women's safety and sexual violence against women in India. It was sparked by the brutal gang rape (and subsequent death) of a young student in Delhi by six men

in December 2012 in Delhi. As someone who spent a lot of my childhood years in Delhi, I felt deeply angry and disgusted, not just by the crime, but by how so many bloody hypocrites came crawling out of the woodwork, politicians, journalists and so called activists, who made it seem like women are somehow to blame for this terrible state of affairs.

A Little Mayhem is the story of a woman who decides to fight back and take the law into her own hands when her sister is raped and killed in a nightclub and she is unable to get justice due to a corrupt police and deeply biased social norms. It's been out on the Kindle for just a few days, so not much reaction yet, but the paperback will be out in India in the coming months with a leading Indian publisher, and I do hope that far from being controversial, it helps spark debate about the horrors so many Indian women have to endure and how our system fails them. To put my money where my mouth is, I've decided to donate my entire advance for the book to a non-profit organization that helps empower women who are victims of violence and abuse.

*You also have an audio book of Zombiestan: A Zombie Novel out on Audible.co.uk. How did that come about and was it a fun project to undertake?*

It was my first experience of having one of my books turned into an audiobook, and it came about when I was approached by the publishers (Tantor) for the rights. The narrator (John Lee) did such a fantastic job that when I heard it for the first time, I felt like he was breathing life into my characters in a way that mere words could not.

*Can you tell us a little about the next book you have planned?*

Right now am working on Book 6 of the Alice in Deadland series. Also, am about to sign the TV series rights for Alice in Deadland to a New York based studio, and am really excited to see how that goes. Hopefully viewers in the US (and elsewhere) will shortly be able to experience the world of Alice not just in my books but on their TV screens as well.

*Finally before we let you go. Do you have a piece of advice for our readers who are looking to improve their writing?*

Read a lot, ideally in very different genres so that you get an idea of how others are bringing their craft to life; and of course, keep writing- anything- a column, a diary, short stories, poems, just scribbling your random thoughts, but keep the practice of writing alive each and every day. The more you write, the better you will be, and the more you will understand what kind of writing you truly enjoy and can call your own.

*Thank you again for your time Mainak and we wish you all the best for the future and your up and coming releases.*

Thanks so much!

http://www.mainakdhar.com/

***So, what is your workspace like?***

At the moment, it's a bit of a mess, because I'm decorating one of the rooms so half of my desk is covered with the contents of a book case. That said, I've still got space for my PC and laptop, so it's not too much of a problem. The biggest issue I have is that I'm in a constant battle for desk space with the cat. I love my office space though. I moved to a fairly isolated smallholding in the Brecon Beacons National Park two years ago, and the view out of the window is amazing. If I'm ever struggling with something, I can take a breath, look up and see forests and mountains stretching out across the horizon. It's inspiring and I love having the space without people being around. That said, I have to work away a lot of the time with my day job, so probably half of my last novel was written in hotel rooms. I still would much rather do my writing at home, but really all I need is my laptop and no interruptions.

***Do you have a go-to gadget / app or service that you cannot live without?***

My laptop is the most important device I have. All of my writing gets done on that, even when I'm at home. I do my editing on my desktop PC, because having two monitors makes it much easier to compare drafts, or have notes from my editor open on one screen while I update my manuscript. However, the one thing that I find absolutely invaluable is my Dropbox. After I lost a fairly significant chunk of the first novel to a hard drive failure, being able to store my files in one place and access them from any computer is a life saver. I hardly save any files locally anymore, although I do have a pretty rigorous backup routine in place, because after the first data loss catastrophe, I'm determined not to go through it again.

***Do you have a set routine while you work?***

I always start my writing off by reading back the last chapter that I wrote. I find that it helps refresh my memory of what happened last time, and gets me back into the heads of my characters. I'll often tweak little things during that re-read, so my first drafts end up being fairly clean as a result, then I'll just dig in and plough through the next part of the story. I try to write at least one scene a day, and at least one chapter a week, although if I'm in the zone, I'll try and push on for as long as I can. It means that I'm not the fastest, or most prolific writer in the world, but at least I know that I'm chipping away at the story and making progress. I'd love to be able to commit eight hours a day to my writing, but with the demands of the day job, plus the work required to keep a small holding up and running, I can only squeeze a couple of hours a day in at most.

***What is the best piece of advice you have ever received?***

I saw a great quote on Facebook from Joe Lansdale that said
*"Write like everyone you know is dead. Make it personal. It's just for you.*
*And then when it's done you can worry about an audience. No one truly*
*knows what everyone wants or likes."* That's so true. There is no point

in setting out to write a story to fit a certain market, or to jump on the latest genre bandwagon.

Write the sort of thing that you want to read. If you are enjoying the journey, it will come across in what
you are writing. If you are doing something by the numbers, then the chances are that you'll lose interest in it, and that will also be pretty damn obvious in the finished story, if you ever finish it at all.

***Do you have a final piece of advice for our readers?***

If you find yourself hitting a brick wall, or procrastinating, then you are most likely over-thinking things. I find it often happens when I am about to write a big scene. I agonise over it, worrying that I won't be able to do the idea justice. And every time that happens, I find that when I sit down, start writing and let the words flow, the end result is at least as good as I'd hoped. Often better, and sometimes it will surprise me. Planning is all very well, but at some point you need to take yourself out of the picture, let your characters come to life and see where they take you. You can always tidy things up later on. The important thing is to keep churning those words out, even if it sometimes feels like you are swimming in treacle.

**About Graeme Reynolds:**

Graeme Reynolds has been called many things over the years, most of which are unprintable.

By day, he breaks computer programs for a living, but when the sun goes down he hunches over

a laptop and thinks of new and interesting ways to offend people with delicate sensibilities.

He has published over thirty short stories, and his debut novel, High Moor, made the semi-finals of the 2011 Bram Stoker Awards. His latest novel, High Moor 2: Moonstruck, was released in 2013 and seems to be upsetting all of the right people.

He lives somewhere in Wales with two cats, a menagerie of delinquent animals and a girlfriend that is beginning to suspect that there is something deeply wrong with him.


You can find Graeme at the following places:

http://www.graemereynolds.com
http://www.facebook.com/HighMoorNovel
http://www.facebook.com/graeme.reynolds2
@graemereynolds

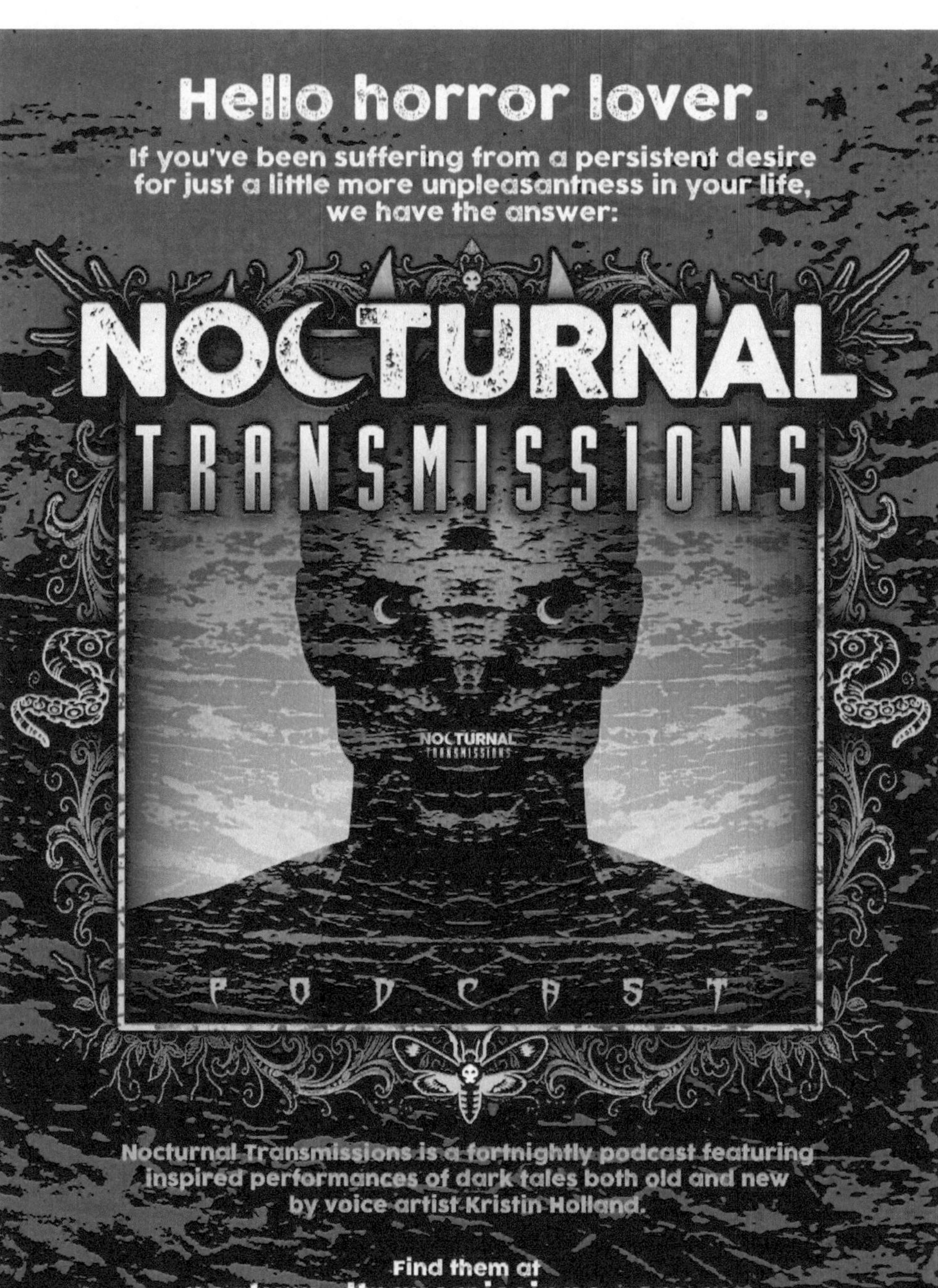

Hello horror lover.
If you've been suffering from a persistent desire
for just a little more unpleasantness in your life,
we have the answer:
NOCTURNAL
TRANSMISSIONS
NOCTURNAL
TRANSMISSIONS
PODCAST
Nocturnal Transmissions is a fortnightly podcast featuring
inspired performances of dark tales both old and new
by voice artist Kristin Holland.
Find them at
nocturnaltransmissions.com.au
or wherever good podcasts are purveyed.

If you have any feedback or would like to leave a review please head over to Amazon and share your thoughts about Sanitarium.

Thank you for your time and we salute your love for all things horror.

www.ingramcontent.com/pod-product-compliance
Lightning Source LLC
Chambersburg PA
CBHW020721160726
47993CB00006B/2290